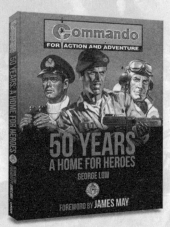

THREE OF THE BEST NORTH AFRICAN DESERT WAR COMMANDO COMIC BOOK ADVENTURES

EDITED BY CALUM LAIRD, EDITOR OF COMMANDO

CARLTON
BOOKS

Published in 2012 by Carlton Books Limited
An imprint of the Carlton Publishing Group
20 Mortimer Street
London
W1T 3JW

COMMANDO is a trademark of and
© DC Thomson & Co. Ltd. 2012
Associated text, characters and artwork
© DC Thomson & Co. Ltd. 2012

A catalogue record for this book is available from the British Library.

ISBN: 978 1 84732 968 4

Printed and bound by CPI Group (UK) Ltd, Croydon, CR0 4YY

Contents

Introduction

The Desert Rats – the nickname of Britain's 8th Army who fought so valiantly in the Second World War. Were they the toughest of all troops? That's a question that would take years to answer. What's certainly true is that the North African desert where they saw much of their action was a harsh environment, often more dangerous than the enemy they faced across the battlefield.

Under that pitiless sun, though, is a place that is a gift for a storyteller. A fluid war fought over vast distances, often hundreds of miles from other forces, never mind any high command, lends itself to swashbuckling heroes and villainous villains of all sides. Larger-than-life characters abound.

And yet Dave Charlton, hero of the tale "Chariot Of War", seems a smaller-than-life character. Never seeming to mix with his comrades, his nose always stuck in a history book, this ex-university lecturer is obviously no warrior. Fortunately, this is Commando world where people are not always what they seem. With the help of a long-dead Egyptian, Dave transforms into a brainy battler who amazes his mates as much as the enemy.

"Oasis Of Death", on the other hand, has almost more big charac-ters than a pocket-sized Commando

CLEARING MINES WAS A NERVE-WRACKING BUSINESS BUT WATCHING AND WAITING WAS NOT EASY EITHER, ESPECIALLY FOR JOE AND ANDY.

I WISH THEY COULD GET A MOVE ON. ALL THIS HANGING ABOUT GIVES ME THE JITTERS.

I KNOW HOW YOU FEEL, MATE.

should be able to hold – a die-hard Nazi, a fighting British sergeant, a warrior Italian and a crazy Arab leader. The British are pitted against the Italians, the German despises both groups, and the Arab seems determined to wipe out everyone… unless the others can work together.

"Fighting Fool" seems very straightforward after that except that the two men doing most of the fighting are on the same side... and would prefer to knock lumps off each other in preference to their enemies. Corporal Mike Braddon and Private Joe Russel are the men in question; men you'd think had enough on their plate taking on the Afrika Korps without fighting each other.

Settle down, turn up the heating and head for the war with the Desert Rats.

Calum G Laird
Commando Editor

EQUIPMENT OF WWII

No.5 DAIMLER ARMOURED CAR

CREW —3
WEIGHT —7 tons
LENGTH —13ft
WIDTH —8ft
HEIGHT —7ft 4ins
SPEED —40mph

ENGINE —90hp Daimler
ARMAMENT —2-pounder gun
Quick-firing 7.9mm machine gun
Bren gun can be mounted on turret rim
ARMOUR —12mm (nearly half an inch) thick

High mobility was the main feature of the Daimler Armoured Car. It could go backwards or forwards through all the gears at high speeds.
Used mainly for reconnaissance duties, this vehicle could get out of trouble fast if it met any tanks — but it could also dish out plenty of trouble when it had to.

CHARIOT OF WAR

THE ITALIANS AND THE GERMANS KNEW THEY WERE IN FOR A HARD WAR WHEN THEY SLUGGED IT OUT WITH THE BRITISH ARMY IN THE NORTH AFRICAN DESERT. BUT NEVER ONCE DID THEY EXPECT THAT THEY'D HAVE TO CONTEND WITH A WARRIOR PHARAOH WHO HAD BEEN DEAD FOR ALMOST 2,000 YEARS...

EGYPT, 1940. A COMPANY OF BRITISH REINFORCEMENTS WAS ON ITS WAY ACROSS THE DESERT TO CHECK A RECENT ITALIAN COUNTER-ATTACK.

CAN'T WAIT FOR A CRACK AT THOSE SPAGHETTI-MUNCHERS, SARGE.

SURE, JACK. AND THERE'LL BE PLENTY MORE BLOKES COMING ALONG THIS WAY IN THE NEXT FEW DAYS TO GIVE US A HAND.

AMONG THE BRITISH WERE SERGEANT JIM ROSS AND HIS MATE, CORPORAL JACK LUCAS, BOTH TOUGH VETERANS.

SOME OF THESE LADS ARE JUST OUT FROM BLIGHTY AND PRETTY GREEN WITH IT.

BUT THEY'RE A KEEN BUNCH. I RECKON THEY'LL DO ALL RIGHT.

JIM ROSS LEANED OVER AND SPOKE TO ONE OF THE NEW MEN – DAVE CHARLTON, AN EX-UNIVERSITY LECTURER WAS BUSY READING A BOOK.

IT'LL BE A BIT DIFFERENT FROM RANGE SHOOTING, LAD. HERE THE TARGETS SHOOT BACK.

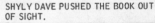

SHYLY DAVE PUSHED THE BOOK OUT OF SIGHT.

SORRY, SARGE, HOW'S THAT AGAIN?

NEVER MIND, CHARLTON. I WAS TALKING TO MYSELF.

LUCAS, WHO FANCIED HE HAD A SHARP EYE FOR MISFITS AMONG THE MEN, PUT IN HIS TUPPENCE WORTH.

THAT DAVE CHARLTON IS A STRANGE BLOKE. HAD HIS NOSE STUCK IN THAT BOOK SINCE WE LEFT BASE.

ALL I EVER READ IS THE SOCCER RESULTS.

THOUGH APPARENTLY ABSORBED IN HIS READING, DAVE WAS THE FIRST TO DETECT THE APPROACHING THROB OF AERO-ENGINES.

EYETIE KITES, SARGE! RIGHT BEHIND US.

A COUPLE OF ITALIAN MACCHI FIGHTERS WERE APPROACHING FROM THE REAR.

UNTIL THAT MOMENT THE JOURNEY HAD GONE SMOOTHLY AND QUIETLY. NOW WITHIN A FEW SECONDS ALL WAS CHAOS.

THERE ARE THE INGLESI PIGS. LET US TEACH THEM A LESSON.

JIM ROSS TORE THE COVER FROM A LEWIS GUN AND LUCAS RUSHED TO HELP.

RIGHT, LET'S GET THEM!

MAKE WAY, BOOKWORM!

ROSS, WITH A BIT OF LUCK AND A LOT OF SKILL, HIT THE FIRST OF THE ITALIAN FIGHTERS, KILLING THE PILOT.

GREAT! YOU GOT HIM, SARGE.

IT'S ALL IN THE FOOT-WORK!

DAVE GRABBED HIS RIFLE AS THE OTHER PLANE HURTLED DOWN. AIMING QUICKLY, HE SNAPPED OFF A ROUND.

DISTURB MY READING, WOULD YOU.

GET DOWN, YOU IDIOT!

HECK, DON'T YOU KNOW A RIFLE'S USELESS AGAINST A KITE?

THEN ROSS SHOUTED IN ASTONISHMENT —

BLIMEY! THE BOOKWORM DID HIT IT — HE'S HIT IT IN THE GUT!

BY A MILLION-TO-ONE CHANCE, DAVE'S SHOT HAD PENETRATED THE MACCHI'S ENGINE-COWLING.

HAVING SUSTAINED NO SERIOUS DAMAGE, THE CONVOY RESUMED ITS JOURNEY, BUT ROSS HAD A WORD OF ADVICE FOR DAVE.

THAT WAS JUST A LUCKY SHOT, CHARLTON. DON'T PRESS YOUR LUCK IN FUTURE.

NOTHING VENTURED, NOTHING GAINED, SARGE.

DAVE WAS WORRIED IN CASE THEIR POSITION HAD BEEN REPORTED BY THE MACCHI FIGHTER WHICH ESCAPED.

THE KITE I HIT DIDN'T CRASH, SARGE. MAYBE WE SHOULD TAKE A LOOK AROUND.

NOT LIKELY! I CAN SEE THE O.C.'s FACE WHEN I SUGGEST THAT. HE'D BURST A BLOOD VESSEL IF WE WASTED A MINUTE.

IN FACT THE STRICKEN MACCHI HAD CRASH-LANDED ONLY A FEW MILES AWAY AND ITS JUBILANT PILOT WAS REPORTING THE BRITISH CONVOY ROUTE TO THE OFFICER IN COMMAND OF AN ITALIAN ARMOURED UNIT.

WE CAN INTERCEPT IT HERE, AT THE KURGHA PASS, THANKS TO YOUR IN-FORMATION. YOU HAVE DONE WELL.

THANK YOU, MAJOR.

MEANWHILE JACK LUCAS WAS TRYING TO DRAW DAVE OUT OF HIS HABITUAL THOUGHTFUL SILENCE.

I RECKON THAT MUST BE SOME KIND OF MILITARY INSTRUCTION-MANUAL, SEEING YOU'RE SO GOOD WITH A RIFLE.

OH, THAT SHOT WAS SHEER LUCK. BUT IN A WAY YOU'RE RIGHT ABOUT THE BOOK.

I STUDIED ANCIENT EGYPT BEFORE I WAS CALLED UP. THE OLD PHARAOH'S MILITARY STRATEGY AGAINST THE ROMANS WAS MY PET SUBJECT.

AS IF ONE WAR AIN'T ENOUGH!

PHOTMES + WARRIOR PHARAOH

ONCE LAUNCHED ON HIS FAVOURITE SUBJECT, THERE WAS NO STOPPING DAVE.

MATTER OF FACT, THIS CHAP CALLED PHOTMES FOUGHT OVER THIS VERY DESERT TWO THOUSAND YEARS AGO. NOBODY KNOWS IF HE WON OR NOT.

THE O.C., MAJOR STUART, STOPPED THE CONVOY JUST AS IT ENTERED THE KURGHA PASS. DARKNESS WAS FALLING AND SENTRIES WERE POSTED.

SENTRIES ON ALL HIGH POINTS, AND NO FIRES. WE'LL MOVE OUT AT DAWN.

YES, SIR.

THE MEN WERE FACED WITH THE UNATTRACTIVE PROSPECT OF COLD FOOD AS THE CHILL DESERT NIGHT ENVELOPED THEM.

BUT THE BRITISH WERE BLISSFULLY UNAWARE OF THE HOT RECEPTION BEING PLANNED FOR THEM FURTHER UP THE PASS.

YOU WILL SILENCE THE INGLESI GUARDS. OUR CARS WILL ATTACK ON YOUR SIGNAL.

SI. RELY ON US, MAJOR.

MEANWHILE THE BRITISH HAD SETTLED DOWN FOR THE NIGHT — ALL EXCEPT DAVE, THAT WAS.

WHAT THE HECK'S CHARLTON DOING, WANDERING ABOUT LIKE THAT?

ROUSING LUCAS, ROSS FOLLOWED DAVE AMONG THE SCATTERED ROCKS THAT LINED THE PASS.

YOU DON'T RECKON HE'S SLEEP-WALKING, DO YOU?

SLEEP-WALKING OR NOT, HE'S DISOBEYING ORDERS.

THE SERGEANT'S BOOMING VOICE INTERRUPTED DAVE'S STUDIOUS CONCENTRATION.

GET BACK TO CAMP BEFORE I PUT YOU ON A CHARGE!

OH, SARGE...I JUST THOUGHT I MIGHT FIND SOME RELICS. THERE'S USUALLY SPEAR-HEADS AND THINGS ON THE SITES OF ANCIENT BATTLES.

DAVE GUESSED THE BITTER TRUTH.

THEY KILLED OUR SENTRIES AND THEY'RE ATTACKING THE REST OF THE CONVOY.

AND WE CAN'T LIFT A FINGER TO HELP THEM.

THAT'S RIGHT, AMICI.

WAS IT NOT A BRILLIANT PLAN? OUR GUNS ARE CUTTING YOUR FRIENDS TO PIECES.

KEEP TALKING, MATE...

AND IN THAT UNGUARDED MOMENT AS THE ITALIAN LOOKED TOWARDS THE GUNFLASHES ROSS LASHED OUT.

TAKE THAT, YOU RAT!

UGH!

EVEN AS ROSS STRUCK, BACK AT THE CAMP, MAJOR STUART MADE HIS DECISION.

OK, LADS — WE'VE HAD IT! CEASE FIRING.

WHEN DAVE AND HIS COMPANIONS LOOKED DOWN ON THE KURGHA PASS THE SURVIVING BRITISH HAD RAISED THEIR HANDS IN SURRENDER.

STUART'S THROWN IN THE TOWEL — TO A PACK OF FLAMIN' SPAGHETTI-MUNCHERS!

YOU CAN'T BLAME HIM. IT'S BETTER THAN LETTING MEN DIE USELESSLY. GOOD LEADERS HAVE DONE IT ALL THROUGH HISTORY.

THOUGH OBVIOUSLY UNABLE TO TAKE ON THE SUPERIOR ITALIAN FORCE, THE TRIO COULD RECCE THE SITUATION.

THEY'RE NOT GOING TO TALK ENGLISH FOR OUR BENEFIT, SO WE'LL BE NONE THE WISER IF WE HEAR ANY-THING.

I WAS ONCE ON A DIG IN ITALY AND I PICKED UP A LITTLE OF THE LINGO. YOU TWO CAN COVER ME WHILE I GET INTO EAR-SHOT.

WHILE THE HAPLESS BRITISH PRISONERS WERE DRIVEN OFF, DAVE INCHED NEARER THE ITALIANS.

I WANT ALL TRACES OF THE ACTION ERASED. WE WILL REMAIN NEAR THE PASS, UNDER COVER TO AWAIT THE NEXT BRITISH TRUCKS.

YES, SIR.

CAUTIOUSLY DAVE BEGAN TO MOVE BACK. HE HAD HEARD ENOUGH. THEN THE ITALIAN LIEUTENANT POINTED TO AN EGYPTIAN TOMB NEARBY, EXPOSED NOW WITH ROCK FALLEN AWAY FROM THE FRONT OF IT.

BUT WE CANNOT HIDE THAT, SIR. OUR GUNS MUST HAVE DISLODGED TONS OF THOSE ROCKS.

THEN WE MUST HOPE THE INGLESI DO NOT NOTICE IT.

ROSS AND LUCAS WATCHED DAVE'S STEALTHY PROGRESS ANXIOUSLY FROM THE COVER OF THE ROCKS.

ANOTHER FEW YARDS AND HE'S HOME...

WHAT'S HE PLAYING AT THERE?

SUDDENLY DAVE SEEMED TO FORGET HIS PERILOUS SITUATION AS HE SPOTTED SOMETHING IN THE SAND.

ROSS AND LUCAS WATCHED AGHAST AS DAVE RAN INTO THE OPEN TOWARDS AN ANCIENT STONE WRITING TABLET HALF-BURIED IN THE SAND. BUT TWO ITALIANS HAD ALSO SEEN HIM.

OVER THERE – INGLESI!

DAVE SNATCHED THE STONE TABLET AND WEAVED AND DODGED FOR COVER AS HIS TWO COMPANIONS RAN TO HIS AID.

THE CRAZY FOOL! HE'S NOT RIGHT IN THE HEAD!

HIS HEAD'LL BE FULL OF HOLES IF HE DOESN'T GET DOWN.

FINALLY DAVE REACHED COVER, MIRACULOUSLY UNHURT.

YOU MUST BE MAD, RISKING YOUR NECK FOR THAT JUNK. GIVE ME MY TOMMY GUN – QUICK!

JUNK? THIS IS A PRICELESS FIND, WRITTEN BY A MAN WHO DIED NEARLY TWO THOUS- AND YEARS AGO.

AW, BELT UP!

BUT THE ANCIENT TABLET HAD GIVEN DAVE AN IDEA – AND IT LOOKED LIKE PAYING OFF.

LOOK OVER THERE! MAKE FOR THAT RECESS IN THE WALL.

HARK WHO'S GIVING ORDERS.

DAVE DASHED OVER TO THE HOLLOW IN THE ROCK, AND AS LUCAS GASPED IN AMAZEMENT HE PUSHED HARD AND A ROCK DOOR SWUNG OPEN.

QUICKLY, OVER HERE!

BLIMEY, A DOOR!

IN SECONDS DAVE WAS JOINED IN THE CAVERN BY ROSS AND LUCAS.

HOW THE HECK DID YOU KNOW ABOUT THIS PLACE?

I KNEW PHOTMES' TOMB MUST BE NEAR WHEN I READ ABOUT HIS FUNERAL ON THE TABLET.

IT TOOK A FEW SECONDS FOR THE MEANING OF DAVE'S WORDS TO SINK IN, THEN LUCAS COULD NOT HIDE HIS ASTONISHMENT.

YOU MEAN WE'RE IN A FLIPPIN' GRAVE? BUT I THOUGHT THEY BUILT THOSE PYRAMID THINGS...

YES, BUT NOT ALWAYS.

DAVE GROPED AROUND TILL HE FOUND SOMETHING TO MAKE A TORCH WITH.

MAYBE NOW WE'LL BE ABLE TO FIND ANOTHER WAY OUT.

YOU'D BETTER. WE'LL NEVER GET OUT ALIVE THE WAY WE CAME IN.

AS DAVE HELD THE TORCH ALOFT THEY SAW WALL PAINTINGS, VASES, INSCRIPTIONS, AND PHOTMES' SARCOPHAGUS – EVERYTHING EXACTLY AS IT HAD BEEN LEFT MANY CENTURIES AGO.

GOOD GRIEF! WHAT'S ALL THIS?

THEY USED TO BURY THE PHARAOH'S POSSESSIONS AND THE THINGS HE'D NEED IN THE SPIRIT WORLD. THERE WILL BE ANOTHER WAY OUT OF HERE WHERE HIS SPIRIT WAS SUPPOSED TO GO.

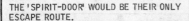

THE 'SPIRIT-DOOR' WOULD BE THEIR ONLY ESCAPE ROUTE.

HELP ME LOOK FOR THE DOOR, IT'LL PROBABLY BE HIGH UP.

I DON'T KNOW HOW YOU CAN TAKE IT SO CALM. THIS PLACE GIVE ME THE CREEPS.

THEN ROSS, WHO HAD BEEN ON LOOK-OUT, SPOKE GRIMLY.

YOU'D BETTER FIND THIS EXIT QUICK. I THINK THE EYETIES ARE GOING TO BLAST US OUT!

ROSS WAS DEAD RIGHT. ALTHOUGH UNABLE TO CARRY OUT THEIR AMBUSH PLAN IF THE BRITISH WERE LEFT TO SOUND A WARNING, THE ITALIANS WERE NOT GOING TO WASTE LIVES WINKLING THEM OUT.

AIM FOR THE WINDOW, BERZONI. ONE SHELL IN THAT CAVE, AND THEY ARE FINISHED.

THE FIRST SHOT WAS ALMOST ON TARGET. LOOSE ROCK SHOWERED DOWN AROUND THE THREE BRITISH.

IT WON'T TAKE THEM LONG TO FIND THE RANGE.

WHAT A WAY TO GO. LIKE TRAPPED RATS...

COME ON, WE CAN GET SOME KIND OF SHELTER BEHIND THIS.

PHOTMES' TOMB, WHICH HAD SEEMED TO OFFER SAFETY, LOOKED LIKE BECOMING A DEATH-CELL. DAVE RACKED HIS BRAINS FOR A SOLUTION TO THEIR PREDICAMENT.

WITH A FIVE-POUNDER FIELD GUN THE ITALIANS BROUGHT TONS OF ROCK DOWN FROM THE OVERHANG, SEALING THE TOMB ENTRANCE BEHIND A MOUNTAIN OF RUBBLE.

ROSS HIT THE PANIC-STRICKEN LUCAS ROUGHLY TO BRING HIM TO HIS SENSES.

LUCAS NOW CALMED, THE THREE MEN SEARCHED FOR A WAY OUT.

THE LID OF PHOTMES' TOMB HAD BEEN SHAKEN LOOSE BY THE ITALIAN SHELLS. THEY LEVERED IT ASIDE, AND AS THEY STARED AT THE EXPOSED MUMMY-CASE THEY HAD A DISTINCTLY EERIE FEELING.

BY GOLLY, THE OLD BOY SEEMS TO BE STARING AT SOMETHING UP THERE.

I WONDER...

AS ROSS SPOKE DAVE'S EYES FOLLOWED THOSE OF THE PAINTED FACE.

DAVE URGED HIS PUZZLED COMPANIONS TO HELP HIM UP ONTO A HIGH LEDGE WHICH RAN ALL AROUND THE TOMB.

WHERE THE HECK ARE YOU GOING?

JUST FOLLOWING A HUNCH, SARGE.

TO THE OTHERS' AMAZEMENT DAVE PUSHED OPEN A CONCEALED TRAP-DOOR IN THE ROOF.

GREAT! THIS IS WHAT I WAS HOPING FOR.

IN SECONDS LUCAS AND ROSS WERE UP ON THE LEDGE AND DAVE WAS HOISTING HIMSELF THROUGH THE OPENING IN THE ROOF.

I DON'T UNDERSTAND IT, CHARLTON. YOU'D THINK SOMEONE WAS GUIDING YOU, THE WAY YOU FIND YOUR WAY ABOUT.

THE TRAP-DOOR LED TO A LONG PASSAGE LINED WITH STATUES OF PHOTMES. THEY FOLLOWED ON, HOPING IT WOULD LEAD TO SAFETY, DAVE STILL CLUTCHING THE TABLET HE HAD FOUND.

SOON THEY REACHED THE END OF THE PASSAGEWAY, BUT IT LOOKED LITERALLY LIKE A DEAD END.

UNCANNILY DAVE'S HAND WENT TO A BLOCK OF STONE FIXED AGAINST THE WALL. HE PUSHED DOWN AND TO THE OTHERS'ASTONISHMENT A CONCEALED EXIT OPENED IN THE ROCKS.

THEY EMERGED INTO BLINDING SUNSHINE HIGH ABOVE THE KURGHA PASS.

THEY DISCOVERED THEY WERE DIRECTLY ABOVE THE ENCAMPED ITALIANS.

THEY'LL BE WAITING TO HIT THE NEXT LOAD OF OUR BLOKES AND THERE'S NOTHING WE CAN DO TO STOP 'EM.

I DON'T KNOW ABOUT THAT, SARGE. TAKE A LOOK HERE.

ONCE AGAIN DAVE REFERRED TO THE WRITING TABLET.

LISTEN, THIS TELLS HOW PHOTMES ONCE STOLE ROMAN HORSES TO MOUNT HIS OWN TROOPS. DOESN'T THAT GIVE YOU AN IDEA?

SURE! WE COULD NICK ONE OF THE EYETIES' ARMOURED CARS.

YOU'RE BOTH CRAZY... BUT IT MIGHT JUST WORK.

IF PHOTMES COULD DO IT, SO CAN WE!

AS THEY WAITED FOR DARKNESS, DAVE TRIED HIS BEST TO DECIPHER THE WRITINGS ON THE TABLET.

I WONDER IF PHOTMES WROTE THIS HIMSELF...

AS DAVE READ OF PHOTMES' LIFE, THE PAST CAME VIVIDLY ALIVE FOR HIM.

IF WE ARE TO DRIVE OUT THE ROMANS, WE MUST BECOME TRUE SOLDIERS, MY FRIENDS. AND WE NEED A LEADER — A GENERAL.

PHOTMES, YOU SHALL LEAD US TO VICTORY.

PHOTMES WAS IN THE THICK OF EVERY BATTLE, FLANKED BY HIS TWO LOYAL LIEUTENANTS, KARNAM AND RAMETH.

ONWARD, FRIENDS. MAKE THEM PAY DEARLY FOR EVERY PIECE OF EGYPTIAN SOIL THEY HAVE STOLEN.

PHOTMES WAGED A GUERILLA WAR, STRIKING HARD AND DISAPPEARING SWIFTLY. SOON HE HAD AN ARMY OF SEASONED FIGHTERS.

ALREADY WE HAVE LEFT OUR MARK ON THE ENEMY.

IT IS DUE TO YOUR LEADERSHIP, PHOTMES.

NO, IT IS NOT ALL MY DOING. AND THERE IS YET A LONG WAY TO GO BEFORE WE WILL BE RID OF THE INVADER.

BUT SOON IT WAS TIME FOR DAVE'S OWN GUERILLA FORCE TO GO INTO ACTION.

COME ON, MATE, THIS WAS YOUR IDEA.

OH, YES. I'LL BE RIGHT WITH YOU.

BY NOW ROSS WAS FULLY OCCUPIED WITH THE PROBLEM OF GETTING TRANSPORT.

THERE'S BOUND TO BE SENTRIES, SO LEAVE THEM TO ME.

SOON THEY REACHED THE ITALIAN CAMP AND, AS ROSS PREDICTED, IT WAS WELL-GUARDED.

GIVE ME TWO MINUTES TO WORK MY WAY BEHIND HIM, THEN TAP THAT ROCK WITH YOUR GUN.

OK, SARGE.

ROSS WAS IN POSITION AT THE OTHER SIDE OF THE PASS WELL WITHIN THE TIME HE'D SET.

ANY SECOND NOW...

AS LUCAS TAPPED THE ROCK, THE SENTRY TURNED.

GOOD, HE'S LOOKING ROUND.

AT LAST DAVE TRIUMPHANTLY HELD UP THE WRITING TABLET.

GOT IT. LET'S GO!

HURRY UP, YOU CRACKPOT.

THEY CLAMBERED ABOARD THE VEHICLE.

WE'LL JUST HAVE TO HOPE THIS ONE'S GOT A FULL TANK.

IF IT DOESN'T, IT'LL BE TOO BAD.

THE ARMOURED CAR WAS WELL OUT OF RANGE BEFORE THE ITALIANS STUMBLED FROM THEIR SLEEP.

WHAT IS GOING ON? GET AFTER THAT CAR!

THE CAPTURED VEHICLE SPED THE THREE JUBILANT BRITISH ACROSS TRACKLESS DESERT.

I NEVER THOUGHT WE'D DO IT — BUT IT WAS YOUR IDEA, CHARLTON.

NO, OLD PHOTMES THOUGHT OF IT FIRST!

BY MORNING THEY WERE WELL AWAY FROM THE KURGHA PASS AND THE ITALIANS, WHO COULD SPARE LITTLE TIME SEARCHING FOR THEM.

AS DAVE TOLD THE STORY TO ROSS AND LUCAS THEY LEARNED HOW PHOTMES HAD ACCEPTED HIS FIRST DEFEAT.

INSTEAD OF FLEEING, HE FOUND AND FOLLOWED THE ROUTE TAKEN BY THE VICTORIOUS ROMANS.

IT SAYS MUCH FOR US THAT SO MANY OF THE ENEMY DIED OF WOUNDS.

IT IS LUCKY FOR US, TOO.

IN MINUTES HE AND HIS FRIENDS HAD DONNED ROMAN UNIFORMS.

OUR ONLY HOPE IS TO RELEASE OUR MEN WHO WERE CAPTURED. OTHERWISE WE WILL REMAIN GENERALS WITHOUT AN ARMY.

CLAD IN THE UNIFORM OF THEIR ENEMIES, PHOTMES AND HIS FRIENDS MARCHED BOLDLY PAST THE ROMAN GUARDS WHEN THEY REACHED THE ROMAN CAMP.

SHOW US WHERE THE PRISONERS ARE BEING KEPT, MAN.

AT ONCE, SIR.

THE EGYPTIAN PRISONERS WERE WELL-GUARDED, BUT PHOTMES WAS COUNTING ON THE ELEMENT OF SURPRISE.

I BEAR ORDERS TO TAKE THE FITTEST OF THESE EGYPTIAN DOGS FOR LABOURERS ON THE NEW ROAD.

TAKE THEM, BUT WATCH THEM CLOSELY. THESE MEN ARE DANGEROUS.

THEN PHOTMES THREW CAUTION TO THE WIND AND PLAYED HIS HAND. HE HAD BANKED ON HIS APPEARANCE REKINDLING THE FIGHTING SPIRIT OF HIS MEN.

RISE UP, MY GALLANT SOLDIERS, AND SLAY THE ROMANS.

PHOTMES! IT IS PHOTMES!

PHOTMES' PLAN WORKED. HIS APPEARANCE GAVE THE EGYPTIANS NEW HEART.

DIE, ROMAN PIG!

AAGH!

THE AMAZED ROMANS HAD NOT EXPECTED A MASS BREAK-OUT. PHOTMES HAD SAVED THE NUCLEUS OF HIS ARMY TO BEGIN THE FIGHT AGAIN.

ONCE MORE YOU TRIUMPH, PHOTMES.

IT WAS A STROKE OF LUCK THAT DID IT — AND THE ROMANS' STUPIDITY.

ROSS'S SHOUT AS HE SPOTTED SOMETHING IN THE SAND JERKED DAVE'S ATTENTION FROM THE FASCINATING TALE.

LOOK, TYRE TRACKS! THEY'RE PRETTY FRESH TOO.

COULD BE ENEMY TRUCKS — I WOULDN'T LIKE TO BET EITHER WAY.

BUT ONE LOOK WAS ENOUGH FOR ROSS.

THESE TRACKS WERE MADE BY BRITISH TRUCKS. I KNOW THE TYRE TREADS.

HOLD YOUR HORSES. THERE'S BEEN NO BRITISH TRUCKS EXCEPT OURS IN THIS AREA. I RECKON THE ITALIANS USED THEM TO TAKE OUR LADS TO A PRISON CAMP.

WELL, DON'T WASTE TIME. WE'RE STILL MILES FROM H.Q.

WHY DON'T WE FOLLOW AND FREE OUR BLOKES? THEN WE'D HAVE ENOUGH MEN TO TAKE ON THOSE ITALIANS.

DAVE'S IDEA HAD BEEN TRIGGERED BY WHAT HE HAD READ OF THE FREEING OF PHOTMES' MEN.

THERE'S SOMETHING IN WHAT HE SAYS, JIM.

ALL RIGHT, WE'LL GIVE IT A TRY.

BUT DAVE WOULD NOT BE DISSUADED.

ROMANS, ITALIANS, WHAT'S THE ODDS? WHY DON'T WE USE EYETIE UNIFORMS?

AND WHERE DO WE GET THEM?

LUCAS BUTTED IN —

WAIT A MINUTE. THEY WOULD PROBABLY CARRY SPARE KIT IN THAT CAR.

A QUICK SEARCH UNEARTHED A TIN TRUNK CONTAINING THREE ITALIAN UNIFORMS.

HOW'S THIS FOR STARTERS?

SOON THEY HAD DONNED THE ENEMY UNIFORMS, DAVE MASQUERADING AS A MAJOR, LUCAS AND ROSS AS A PRIVATE AND CORPORAL. BUT THE MOST DANGEROUS PART OF THE PLAN WAS STILL TO COME.

WELL, HERE GOES...

WITH CAREFULLY THOUGHT-OUT SENTENCES AND IN HIS BEST ACCENT, DAVE USED HIS KNOWLEDGE OF ITALIAN TO BLUFF HIS WAY PAST THE GUARD.

LET ME PASS. I HAVE ORDERS TO SELECT SOME OF THE PRISONERS FOR A LABOUR FORCE.

VERY WELL, SIR.

DAVE KEPT UP HIS 'INSPECTION' FOR TEN MINUTES, THEN —

UP WITH YOUR HANDS! DON'T TRY ANY FUNNY TRICKS.

DIO MIO!

THE CAMP ERUPTED INTO FURY AS THE BRITISH ATTACKED THEIR GUARDS ON DAVE'S SIGNAL.

AAGH!

IF I CAN GET IN THAT CAR, I MIGHT FINISH THIS A BIT QUICKER.

LEAVING THE ITALIAN GUARDS TO THE TENDER MERCIES OF THE BRITISH PRISONERS, DAVE DASHED FOR THE ARMOURED CAR.

QUICKLY HE CLAMBERED INTO THE TURRET.

IF I CAN FIRE THIS GUN, THE EYETIES WILL THROW IN THE TOWEL.

ROSS AND LUCAS WERE PUZZLED BY DAVE'S DISAPPEARANCE BUT HAD LITTLE TIME TO INVESTIGATE.

WHERE THE HECK IS CHARLTON?

I SAW HIM HEADING FOR THE TIN CAN...

SUDDENLY A DEADLY CHATTER SPLIT THE AIR, AND A HAIL OF BULLETS SWEPT THE CROWDED COMPOUND AS A SECOND ARMOURED CAR, THIS TIME MANNED BY ITALIANS, APPEARED.

BLUE BLAZES!

THE CREW MUST HAVE HELD FIRE EARLIER IN CASE THEY HIT THEIR OWN BLOKES.

IN MINUTES THE REMAINING ITALIANS WERE OVERPOWERED AND DAVE WAS THE HERO OF THE DAY.

WELL DONE, MATE. COULDN'T HAVE DONE BETTER MYSELF.

DON'T LAY IT ON TOO THICK, SARGE. YOU'LL MAKE ME BLUSH.

AFTER THE CONGRATULATIONS, IT WAS DOWN TO SERIOUS WORK.

THIS BLOKE WAS CAPTURED ONLY YESTERDAY AND HE SAYS A BIG CONVOY IS GOING THROUGH THE KURGHA PASS TOMORROW.

AND THEY'LL RUN SMACK INTO THE ITALIANS GUNS UNLESS WE CAN DO SOMETHING ABOUT IT.

THE ITALIANS' ARMOURED CAR WAS RIGHTED AND DAVE DISCLOSED HIS PLAN.

THE TWO ARMOURED CARS CAN ATTACK HEAD-ON WHILE THE MAIN FORCE CLIMBS DOWN BEHIND THE EYETIES.

AND I BET WE'LL BE THE MUGS IN THE CARS!

ALTHOUGH HAVING NO RANK, DAVE SPOKE WITH SUCH AUTHORITY THAT HIS IDEA WAS ACCEPTED.

AFTER DISCARDING THE ITALIAN UNIFORMS DAVE AND THE OTHERS SET OFF, THE TWO CARS LEADING AND A TRUCK WITH THE REST OF THE BRITISH BRINGING UP THE REAR. A FEW HOURS LATER, THE KURGHA PASS WAS IN SIGHT.

THERE'S THE PASS. I HOPE WE'RE IN TIME.

THE PASS WAS REACHED AND IT WAS TIME TO SPLIT UP.

SARGE, TAKE THE OTHER BLOKES IN THE BACK DOOR WHILE JACK AND I GO IN THE FRONT.

NOW, WAIT...

DAVE BROKE IN —

LOOK, I'M ONLY A PRIVATE. BLOKES ALWAYS FOLLOW THE MAN WITH THE STRIPES AND THAT'S YOU, SARGE.

ROSS LED THE MAIN FORCE OVER THE ROCKY SLOPES AS LUCAS AND DAVE WAITED TO CHARGE.

WE'LL GIVE THEM A FEW MORE MINUTES, THEN WE'LL GO.

READY WHEN YOU ARE, MATE.

THE CAR-DRIVERS WHEELED ABOUT AND DODGED THE ITALIANS' FIRE AS DAVE AND LUCAS KEPT THE ENEMIES' HEADS DOWN.

WE CAN'T KEEP THIS UP FOR LONG!

AT THAT CRUCIAL MOMENT ROSS AND THE OTHERS ATTACKED FROM THE REAR.

FOLLOW ME, LADS. WE'VE A DATE TO KEEP WITH A COUPLE OF ARMOURED CARS.

AAGH!

BUT THE FIRST ARMOURED CAR THEY RAN INTO WAS NOT A FRIENDLY ONE.

THE ATTACK WAS IN DANGER OF FAILING IF THE ITALIAN MAJOR'S ARMOURED CAR DROVE BACK THE ATTACK AT THE REAR — UNLESS DAVE AND LUCAS DID SOMETHING ABOUT IT.

DAVE LEANT OUT OF HIS TURRET AND GRABBED A LIVE GRENADE FROM AN ASTONISHED ITALIAN.

DAVE'S CAR SPED UP ABREAST OF THE ITALIAN MAJOR'S WHICH HAD BEEN ATTACKING ROSS AND HIS MEN. HE TOSSED THE GRENADE INTO ITS TURRET WITHOUT HESITATION.

THE STRICKEN ARMOURED CAR TRUNDLED TO A HALT AS ROSS AND HIS MEN EMERGED FROM COVER.

WITHOUT THEIR COMMANDER TO RALLY THEM, THE REMAINING ITALIANS SOON THREW IN THE TOWEL.

EQUIPMENT OF WWII

No.1 TWENTY-FIVE POUNDER GUN

AMMUNITION TRAILER — HOLDS 32 ROUNDS

RECOIL 914mm

SIGHTING GEAR

FIRING LEVER

GUN-LAYER'S SEAT

PRONGS IN GROUND

ELEVATING HAND-WHEEL

TRAVERSING HAND-WHEEL

SHIELD   OPEN SIGHT

BATTERY FOR LIGHTING SIGHT

THE GUN GETS ITS NAME
FROM THE WEIGHT
OF THE SHELL —
25 POUNDS (11.34kg)

TWENTY-FIVE POUNDER ON THE MOVE

The British twenty-five pounder gun was perhaps the best general purpose heavy gun of World War II. Equally useful in defence or attack, the twenty-five pounder (calibre 87mm) was found to be especially effective against German tanks. With its high elevation it could seek out enemy targets supposedly safely hidden and sheltered in deep, low-lying cover. Very mobile, once coupled to the strange-looking vehicle called a "Quad" which towed it, the gunners could take it any place, any time, at high speed.

OASIS OF DEATH

A MAD ARAB LEADER, DETERMINED TO SLAUGHTER ALL BRITISH SOLDIERS...
A CAPTURED BATTLE-FLAG, PROUDEST POSSESSION OF THE REGIMENT...
A YOUNG SERGEANT, SENT OUT INTO THE DESERT TO DIE...
AND THE OASIS OF DEATH HELD THE SECRET OF THEM ALL.

IT ALL BEGAN IN 1884 WHEN QUEEN VICTORIA SAT ON THE BRITISH THRONE, RULER OF THE GREATEST EMPIRE IN THE WORLD. BUT IN THAT EVENTFUL YEAR, DISCONTENT WAS ALREADY WIDESPREAD IN AFRICA, AND WHEN MOHAMMED AHMED ASSUMED THE TITLE "MAHDI" — THE PROPHET — HE SET LIGHT TO A SEETHING REBELLION THAT FLARED THROUGH THE SUDAN,

BUT THE SCREAMING DERVISHES WHO FOUGHT FOR THE MAHDI WERE NO ORDINARY WARRIORS, AS THE BRITISH WERE TO FIND OUT TO THEIR COST.

SLOWLY, FIGHTING EVERY INCH OF THE WAY, THE BRITISH UNWILLINGLY GAVE GROUND, UNTIL THE INCREDIBLE HAPPENED - THEY BROKE! COLOUR SERGEANT "TUG" WILSON, IRON-HARD VETERAN OF THE AFGHAN WARS, SAW THE WILD-EYED DERVISHES STRUGGLE TO REACH HIM. THEY WERE AFTER THE REGIMENT'S COLOUR.

THE COLOUR! RALLY TO THE COLOUR!

GRIMLY HE TORE THE PRECIOUS COLOUR FROM THE STAFF AS THE SCREAMING NATIVES MOVED EVEN CLOSER.

AWAY WITH YOU, YOU DEVILS! YOU HAVEN'T GOT ME BEATEN YET!

FOR FIVE MORE INCREDIBLE MINUTES HE WITHSTOOD THE FULL FURY OF THE DERVISH ATTACK, UNTIL SHEER WEIGHT OF NUMBERS BORE HIM TO THE GROUND. ONLY WHEN HIS SENSES LEFT HIM DID THE ENEMY SEIZE HIS FLAG, AND RUSH AWAY WITH IT IN UNHOLY TRIUMPH.

NOW WE HAVE THE BANNER OF THE UNBELIEVERS!

IT WAS ONE OF THE FEW TIMES IN HISTORY THAT A BRITISH SQUARE HAD BROKEN — BUT THE DERVISHES HAD PAID A HEAVY PRICE FOR THEIR SUCCESS.

EVEN ALTHOUGH THE FOLLOWING YEAR WOULD SEE THE CRUSHING OF THE MAHDI'S FORCES, THIS HAD BEEN ONE DAY WHERE THE FORCES OF ISLAM HAD TRIUMPHED. THE BATTERED SURVIVORS OF THE BRITISH FORCE WERE MARCHED OFF TO CAPTIVITY.

WHAT'LL HAPPEN TO US NOW?

DON'T ASK ME. I RECKON WE'VE HAD IT. I SAW 'EM BUTCHER OLD TUG WILSON, TOO. COO, WHAT A FIGHT HE PUT UP!

BUT THE IRON-HARD COLOUR SERGEANT WAS VERY FAR FROM DEAD — AS A BRITISH RELIEVING FORCE DISCOVERED THE NEXT MORNING.

SIR! THIS ONE'S STILL BREATHING!

HE MUST BE TOUGH AS NAILS.

TUG WILSON WAS ONE OF A RARE BREED OF MEN, MEN WHO DIDN'T KNOW THE MEANING OF DEFEAT, WHO CLUNG TO THE SPARK OF LIFE DESPITE ALL ODDS.

SO THEY GOT THE COLOUR. WELL, I'LL SAY THIS FOR 'EM — THEY EARNED IT, THEM DEVILS!

LIE DOWN, SARGE. YOU'VE LOST A FAIR DROP O' BLOOD IN THIS DUST-UP.

COLOUR SERGEANT TUG WILSON HAD LIVED TO FIGHT ANOTHER DAY — AND TO BRING UP A FAMILY. SO IT WASN'T REALLY SURPRISING THAT HIS GRANDSON DAVID WENT BACK TO THE DESERT IN 1941, FOR THE WILSONS WERE A WARRIOR FAMILY AND THE BRITISH WERE AT WAR AGAIN IN AFRICA.

STAND BY, NOBBY. LOOKS LIKE THE SKIPPER'S SPOTTED SOMETHING.

PRIVATE NOBBY CLARK WAS DAVE'S DRIVER.

A SOLDIER SINCE HE LEFT SCHOOL, DAVE WILSON HAD EAGERLY VOLUNTEERED FOR A MOTORISED RAIDING FORCE OPERATING BEHIND GERMAN LINES, AND HAD SOON BECOME A SERGEANT.

HE WANTS ME UP FRONT. KEEP AN EYE OUT FOR AIRCRAFT, OK?

WILL DO, DAVE, BUT I RECKON WE'RE TOO FAR SOUTH FOR THAT.

LIEUTENANT JACK CAMERON, FROM GLASGOW, WAS IN COMMAND OF THE PATROL.

HAVE A SHUFTI OVER THERE, DAVE. I'LL BET THAT'S ANOTHER POOR DEVIL LIKE THE ONE WE BURIED A COUPLE OF DAYS BACK.

HORRIFIED, DAVE SAW IT WAS AN AUSTRALIAN SOLDIER DRAGGING HIMSELF AIMLESSLY ACROSS THE DUNES. THE MAN WAS IN THE LAST STAGES OF EXHAUSTION.

THEY DASHED ACROSS THE BURNING SANDS TOWARDS HIM. BUT EVEN AS THEY REACHED HIM THE MAN COLLAPSED, STRUGGLING TO SPEAK THROUGH PARCHED, SWOLLEN LIPS. ON HIS BROW WAS TATTOOED A SCIMITAR.

ANOTHER AUSSIE! AND THAT SAME TATTOO MARK — JUST LIKE THE OTHER BLOKE HAD. WHAT GOES ON, SKIPPER?

BUT THEY WERE TOO LATE. THE MAN, OUT OF HIS MIND WITH THIRST, DIED BEFORE HE COULD SPEAK.

SEE IF HE'S GOT ANY IDENTITY DISCS.

HOW DID HE GET AS FAR SOUTH AS THIS? OUR NEAREST UNITS ARE AT LEAST SIXTY MILES AWAY.

JACK CAMERON SHOOK HIS HEAD AS HE GAZED SOUTH OVER THE PARCHED EMPTY SANDS.

THERE'S THE OASIS AT EL SUQ, BUT THERE'S NOTHING THERE APART FROM A FEW BEDOUIN. NO, I RECKON HE RAN INTO SOME HOSTILE ARABS WHO LEFT HIM TO DIE — AFTER THEY'D BRANDED HIM.

THE SMALL PATROL TURNED NORTH, NAVIGATING BY SUN-COMPASS.

TAKE THE LEAD FOR A WHILE, DAVE. I'LL KEEP A CHECK ON YOUR BEARINGS.

OK, SKIPPER. MOVE UP FRONT, NOBBY. AIM FOR THE LEFT OF THAT ESCARPMENT.

THEY HAD ALMOST REACHED THE LANDMARK WHEN KEEN EARS HEARD THE DRONE OF AN APPROACHING AIRCRAFT.

THE FOCKE-WULF WAS DIVING EVEN AS IT PASSED OVER THEM. IF THE PILOT HAD SEEN THEM, THEY COULD EXPECT AN IMMEDIATE ATTACK.

MEANWHILE, THE FIGHTER PILOT, MAJOR ERICH BRUNNER OF THE LUFTWAFFE, SURVEYED HIS NEW SURROUNDINGS. HE WAS NOT IMPRESSED.

WHAT A PLACE! AND NOTHING BUT USELESS GARLIC-EATING ITALIANS FOR COMPANY.

COLONEL UMBERTO MICCA, THE STATION COMMANDER, HAD OVERHEARD BRUNNER'S REMARKS. HE SNAPPED A REPLY.

I AM NOT IGNORANT OF GERMAN, HERR MAJOR. I ASSURE YOU I DO NOT CARE FOR THE ARRANGEMENT EITHER!

PAH! HAD YOUR SO-CALLED LEADER NOT ALLOWED HALF HIS PITIFUL AIR FORCE TO BE BLASTED OUT OF THE SKY, I WOULD NOT BE HERE.

THUS THE TWO RELUCTANT ALLIES MADE EACH OTHER'S ACQUAINTANCE.

THROUGH THE SCORCHING HEAT OF THE AFTERNOON AND EVENING, JACK AND HIS PATROL SAT TIGHT. THEN AT MIDNIGHT, THEY ATTACKED.

INGLESI! INGLESI!

AT BREAK-NECK SPEED THE THREE JEEPS HURTLED DOWN THE DUSTY AIRSTRIP, THEIR MACHINE-GUNS HAMMERING STREAMS OF LEAD AT THE ITALIAN BOMBERS.

DAVE FELT A TREMENDOUS WAVE OF EXCITEMENT SURGING THROUGH HIM AS THEY PELTED THROUGH THE SMOKE AND DUST.

AS SENIOR OFFICER HERE, I WOULD PREFER IT IF YOU TRIED TO SAVE THE AIRCRAFT INSTEAD OF INDULGING IN USELESS INSULTS, BRUNNER. NEVER FEAR — I WILL CATCH THE INGLESI.

THE GERMAN SPAT OUT AN ANSWER.

CATCH THEM? YOU HAVEN'T A CHANCE! BY THE TIME YOU GET AFTER THEM THEY'LL BE IN CAIRO!

BUT THE JEEPS HAD NOT GONE VERY FAR. THE PATROL HAD STOPPED TO REORGANISE, AND JACK CAMERON BEGAN TO WORRY. HE WONDERED IF HE HAD BEEN TOO EAGER IN AGREEING TO ATTACK.

HEY, THEY'RE QUICK OFF THE MARK. SPLIT UP, AND WE'LL RENDEZVOUS TOMORROW AT POINT THIRTY-SIX.

DAVE AND NOBBY HEADED SOUTH-EAST, AND THOUGH THEY DIDN'T KNOW IT THEN, THEY HAD COLONEL UMBERTO MICCA HIMSELF ON THEIR TRAIL, IN A HALF-TRACK FULL OF TOUGH GERMAN SOLDIERS.

THEY ARE SEPARATING. I THOUGHT AS MUCH, OF COURSE. I PERSONALLY WILL SEE TO THAT ONE. GO AFTER HIM!

AT THE AIRSTRIP, BRUNNER WAS TRYING DESPERATELY TO FIND A PLANE — ANY PLANE.

THIS IS THE LEAST DAMAGED, HERR MAJOR, BUT IT WILL TAKE SOME TIME TO GET IT READY...

THEN GET IT READY, QUICKLY!

JACK CAMERON AND STAN HARDY HAD SOON SHAKEN OFF THEIR PURSUERS, BUT MICCA GRIMLY CHASED DAVE AND NOBBY. HE WAS DETERMINED TO MAKE A CAPTURE.

THERE HE IS! FASTER!

MOVE IT, NOBBY, THE BLIGHTERS ARE GAINING!

THE JEEP, ALTHOUGH FASTER THAN THE HALF-TRACK, HAD TO TWIST AND TURN TO AVOID THE SMALL DUNES AND HOLLOWS. THE LARGER VEHICLE CAME STRAIGHT ON OVER EVERYTHING.

DAVE PALED AS LEAD SPATTERED INTO THE SAND A FEW YARDS FROM THE SPEEDING JEEP.

HEY, THAT WAS CLOSE!

HE SWUNG THE JEEP'S MACHINE GUN ROUND AND LOOSED OFF A LONG BURST.

THAT SHOULD KEEP THEIR HEADS DOWN FOR A MINUTE.

THEN NEXT MINUTE A RICOCHETTING ENEMY BULLET HIT NOBBY IN THE HEAD. THE JEEP LURCHED TO A STANDSTILL.

THEY'VE GOT HIM! ALL RIGHT, THEY'VE ASKED FOR IT NOW.

DAVE WAITED IN A DEADLY FURY UNTIL THE HALF-TRACK WAS ONLY A HUNDRED YARDS AWAY. THEN HE LET GO A SAVAGE BURST OF FIRE.

THIS IS FOR NOBBY!

DAVE'S BULLETS WHINED AND SPATTERED ALONG THE METAL SIDE OF THE HALF-TRACK. THE DRIVER GAVE A HOARSE YELL AND TOPPLED OUT OF THE CAB. MICCA SCREAMED OUT IN ANGER.

AAAGH!

STOP THIS THING, SOMEONE! QUICKLY! THE INGLESI WILL PAY FOR THIS!

DRIVERLESS, THE UNGAINLY VEHICLE CHURNED ROUND IN A TIGHT CIRCLE AND STOPPED IN A PATCH OF SOFT SAND. NO SOONER HAD THE DUST SETTLED THAN MICCA WAS SHOUTING AGAIN.

IT SEEMS TO BE STUCK.

I CAN SEE THAT, YOU FOOL. DIG IT OUT! HURRY!

DAVE JUMPED BACK INTO THE JEEP'S DRIVING SEAT. THE IMMEDIATE THREAT WAS OVER. HE WOULD HAVE A CLEAR RUN FOR A WHILE.

THAT'LL KEEP 'EM FOR A BIT! GIVE ME A CHANCE TO GET CLEAR.

AFTER A WHILE HE STOPPED TO BURY NOBBY. IT WAS THEN HE MADE THE STARTLING DISCOVERY THAT THE COMPASS HAD BEEN SMASHED IN THE FIGHT.

THAT'S THE COMPASS GONE. HAVE TO STEER BY THE STARS NOW. NO POINT IN STICKING AROUND HERE, ANYWAY.

HE PRESSED ON, BUT JUST AFTER DAYBREAK A SANDSTORM BLEW UP, BLACKING OUT THE SUN. HE GRITTED HIS TEETH AND URGED THE JEEP FORWARD.

BLAST THIS SAND! I COULD BE GOING ROUND IN CIRCLES FOR ALL I KNOW. STILL, THOSE EYETIES WILL BE JUST AS LOST AS I AM.

BUT IN THIS HE WAS WRONG. MICCA AND HIS MEN HAD MANAGED TO GET THE HALF-TRACK MOVING AGAIN, AND WERE STILL ON HIS TRAIL.

WHEN THE SANDSTORM SUBSIDED, THE JEEP'S TYRE-MARKS HAD DISAPPEARED INTO THE VAST, ANONYMOUS WASTES OF SAND. BUT MICCA REFUSED TO BECOME DISCOURAGED, DESPITE BROAD HINTS FROM THE SOLDIERS.

EL SUQ. WHEN THE STORM CLEARED, DAVE HAD SEEN THE GREEN FRONDS OF PALM TREES IN THE DISTANCE.

WITH MY LUCK, THAT'S PROBABLY A MIRAGE. BUT STILL, I'VE NOTHING TO LOSE, SO LET'S GO.

BUT THE VINDICTIVE MAJOR BRUNNER HAD GOT A FOCKE-WULF AIRBORNE, AND EVEN AS DAVE SPED TOWARDS THE OASIS THE GERMAN SPOTTED HIM.

SO, ENGLANDER — A TASTE OF YOUR OWN MEDICINE, I THINK.

AFTER THE DEVASTATION OF HIS AIRFIELD, BRUNNER WAS IN A FAR FROM FRIENDLY MOOD. HE PUSHED THE STICK FORWARD, HIS THUMB HOVERING OVER THE FIRING BUTTON.

WARNED BY THE SOUND OF THE ENGINE, DAVE SCREAMED TO A HALT IN A CLOUD OF DUST. HE THREW HIMSELF ACROSS TO THE MACHINE GUN.

RIGHT, YOU BLIGHTER, LET'S GET ON WITH IT.

THE FOCKE WULF'S BULLETS LASHED THE SAND WITHIN FEET OF THE JEEP AS BRUNNER FORCED HIS MACHINE INTO A SCREAMING DIVE. GRIMLY, DAVE HELD HIS GROUND AND FIRED BACK.

GET LOST, JERRY!

THEN THE NAZI PULLED BACK AGAIN INTO A TIGHT TURN.

IT WASN'T BRUNNER'S LUCKY DAY. DAVE FIRED JUST AS THE GERMAN SWUNG HIS PLANE ROUND FOR ANOTHER ATTACK.

HIMMEL! MISSED HIM!

ACH!

BRUNNER FELT THE PLANE LURCH AS THE SLUGS HACKED INTO THE FUSELAGE. A BARE SECOND LATER HIS ENGINE COUGHED AND BURST INTO SEARING FLAME.

HE FOUGHT TO CONTROL THE STAGGERING FIGHTER AS THE ENGINE SHUDDERED IN TORMENT. STREAKS OF OIL OVER THE WINDSCREEN MADE IT ALMOST IMPOSSIBLE FOR HIM TO SEE.

TEUFEL! I CAN'T HOLD HER!

DESPITE HIS EFFORTS, HE HADN'T THE HEIGHT TO AVOID A CRASH. HIS AIRSCREW NICKED A LOW DUNE, AND THE FIGHTER PLOUGHED UP A VAST CLOUD OF DUST.

DAVE WATCHED THOUGHTFULLY AS A PLUME OF SMOKE MARKED THE END OF BRUNNER'S PLANE.

WELL, THAT'S THAT. TALK ABOUT SHEER LUCK!

THE OASIS OF EL SUQ LOOKED JUST LIKE A MIRAGE. GHOSTLY WHITE BUILDINGS SHIMMERED THROUGH THE PALM TREES — BUT THERE WAS NO SIGN OF ANY HUMAN BEING.

STRANGE — THERE DOESN'T SEEM TO BE ANYBODY ABOUT. LOOKS DESERTED.

ANY TRACKS THERE MIGHT HAVE BEEN TO THE OASIS HAD BEEN WIPED OUT BY THE SANDSTORM. DAVE DROVE STRAIGHT IN — TO DISASTER.

AS IF AT A GIVEN SIGNAL, FEARSOME EVIL FIGURES MATERIALISED FROM THE FRINGE OF THE OASIS — WARLIKE FIGURES, ARMED WITH RIFLES AND SCIMITARS.

DAVE WAS JUST PICKING HIMSELF UP WHEN BULLETS WHIPPED PAST HIS HEAD. HE DIVED FOR THE GROUND, CLAWING FOR HIS TOMMY GUN.

HEY! EVEN THE ARABS ARE AFTER ME NOW.

GRABBING HIS TOMMY GUN, HE DIVED BEHIND THE JEEP AND CUT LOOSE WITH A QUICK BURST.

AND I THOUGHT THESE JOKERS WERE NEUTRAL!

MICCA HAD HEARD THE SHOTS. HE URGED THE HALF-TRACK FORWARD INTO THE FRAY.

OH, NO, HERE COMES THE WOP! I'VE HAD IT — UNLESS HE HITS THAT MINEFIELD!

LIKE DAVE, MICCA WAS COMPLETELY UNAWARE OF THE MINEFIELD. HE BLUNDERED STRAIGHT ON, WITH SPECTACULAR RESULTS.

MICCA'S MEN HADN'T A CHANCE. SHAKEN AND DAZED BY THE EXPLOSION, MOST OF THEM FELL TO THE NATIVES' FIRE IN A FEW SECONDS.

DAVE WILSON WAS FIRST AND FOREMOST A SOLDIER. FIGHTING ITALIANS AND GERMANS WAS HIS BUSINESS. BUT WHAT RIGHT HAD ANYONE ELSE TO BARGE IN ON A PRIVATE DUST-UP? HE SHOUTED TO THE ITALIAN.

HEY! CAN YOU RUN OVER HERE IF I COVER YOU?

THE ITALIAN'S VOICE CAME BACK FEEBLY.

MY LEGS ARE TRAPPED, I CANNOT MOVE.

DAVE WAS TAKEN ABACK BY MICCA'S ANSWER, BUT HE DID NOT HESITATE —

OK, I'LL COME FOR YOU. KEEP DOWN!

A QUICK BURST OF FIRE KEPT THE ARABS' HEADS DOWN JUST LONG ENOUGH FOR HIM TO REACH MICCA. THE ITALIAN WAS WELL AND TRULY STUCK. ONLY BRUTE FORCE WOULD GET HIM OUT.

THE INBRED TOUGHNESS OF THE WILSONS SHOWED CLEARLY ON THE GRIMLY-DETERMINED FACE — IN THE SINEWY, STRAINING MUSCLES AS DAVE GRAPPLED WITH THE HEAVY TRACK.

INCH BY INCH HE HEAVED AND STRAINED UNTIL FINALLY MICCA CRAWLED OUT ON TO THE SAND, EXHAUSTED.

THANK YOU, INGLESE. FOR HOURS I HUNT YOU DOWN — AND NOW THIS.

FORGET IT, MATE. THAT WAS YOUR JOB. BUT WHAT'S NEEDLING THEM ARABS — THEY GONE MAD OR SOMETHING?

MICCA WAS EVEN MORE AMAZED.

THIS I CANNOT UNDERSTAND. THE ITALIAN ARMY HAS BEEN USING EL SUQ AS A SUPPLY DUMP FOR TWO YEARS. ANYWAY, THEY ARE DERVISHES, NOT ARABS.

WE HAVE PAID THE TRIBE WELL FOR THE PRIVILEGE. IN THERE ARE ITALIAN VEHICLES, ARMS, AND AMMUNITION. THEY WERE FOR OUR GREAT ATTACK ON EGYPT.

THE ONE THAT GENERAL WAVELL STOPPED, EH? WELL, I CAN'T SAY YOUR PALS ARE VERY FRIENDLY NOW!

EVEN AS THEY SPOKE, THE DERVISHES HAD MOVED IN CLOSER. DAVE RAISED HIS GUN AND PRESSED THE TRIGGER. NOTHING HAPPENED.

BLAST IT! OUT OF AMMO. WELL, THAT'S THAT.

RELUCTANTLY THE TWO MEN STOOD UP AND RAISED THEIR HANDS. IMMEDIATELY THEY WERE SURROUNDED BY A RING OF EVIL-LOOKING NATIVES.

AT THAT MOMENT, DAVE NOTICED A SOLITARY FIGURE STAGGERING OVER THE SAND-DUNES TOWARDS THEM. BRUNNER HAD ESCAPED WITH HIS LIFE FROM THE WRECKED PLANE, ONLY TO WALK SLAP-BANG INTO MORE TROUBLE.

HERE'S OUR FLYING FRIEND.

HE WAS QUICKLY SEIZED AND MARCHED INTO THE OASIS ALONG WITH THE OTHERS. TALL, FIERCE-LOOKING DERVISHES NOW THRONGED THE NARROW STREETS, ALL ARMED WITH MODERN WEAPONS.

TWICE BEFORE I HAVE BEEN HERE — BUT NEVER HAVE I SEEN SO MANY ARMED MEN.

LEAVE ME ALONE, YOU FILTHY SAVAGE! I AM AN OFFICER OF THE REICH!

MINUTES LATER THEY WERE BEING TAKEN INTO THE LARGEST HOUSE IN THE VILLAGE. AND EVEN AS THEY ENTERED, DARK, EVIL EYES WERE ALREADY WATCHING THEM. AND IN THOSE EYES SHONE NOT ONLY THE SAVAGERY OF WARRING ANCESTORS, BUT THE GLINT OF MADNESS. SHEIK HASSAN AHMED WAS MAD — FOR POWER!

THIS IS SHEIK HASSAN AHMED'S HOUSE. I HAVE BEEN HERE BEFORE — AS AN HONOURED GUEST.

HE WILL SUFFER FOR THIS! THE AFRIKA KORPS WILL CRUSH HIM AND HIS FOLLOWERS LIKE INSECTS WHEN THEY HEAR OF THIS.

DAVE WAS GETTING PRETTY FED UP OF BRUNNER'S MOANING.

OH, PACK IT IN, FRITZ. THERE'S BOUND TO BE AN ANSWER TO THIS CAPER. LET'S JUST WAIT AND SEE.

YOU ARE WISE, ENGLISHMAN, WAIT AND SEE. I TOO HAVE WAITED FOR MANY YEARS. NOW — WE SHALL SEE!

MICCA BURST INTO RAPID ITALIAN, BUT WAS CUT OFF SHORT.

SHEIK HASSAN AHMED! PERCHE —

QUIET, ITALIAN DOG! WE WILL SPEAK ENGLISH. IT IS A CIVILISED LANGUAGE!

IN ANY LANGUAGE YOU ARE A SAVAGE.

DAVE GAPED. THE MAN COULDN'T BE SERIOUS.

YOU'RE GOING TO TAKE ON THE BRITISH AND THE JERRIES, AND WHAT'S LEFT OF THE EYE-TIES, JUST LIKE THAT?

I RESENT THAT! THE DUCE'S ARMY IS STILL A FORCE TO BE RECKONED WITH.

BUT AS THE SHEIK TALKED, IT BECAME CLEAR HE HAD MADE NO IDLE BOAST. HE TOLD OF THE WEALTH THEY HAD BUILT UP BY SLAVE-TRADING. HIS SONS HAD BEEN SENT TO SCHOOL IN EUROPE TO LEARN AND STORE UP KNOWLEDGE — IN READINESS FOR THE NEXT HOLY WAR.

AND I, HASSAN AHMED, AM THE CHOSEN EL MAHDI! ONCE OUR WARRIORS BROKE THE BRITISH RANKS. NOW WE WILL BREAK ALL INFIDELS!

THEN HE LED THEM TO THE NORTH OF THE OASIS. THERE AN ASTOUNDING SIGHT MET THEIR EYES.

A RELIC OF ANCIENT CULTURES. THIS IS THE TEMPLE OF SOBK. COVERED BY SAND FOR THOUSANDS OF YEARS. BUT I HAVE A BETTER USE FOR IT.

AS THEY ENTERED THE GLOOMY PASSAGE, FLAMING TORCHES CAST WEIRD SHADOWS.

YOU WILL SOON SEE WHY I NEED TRAINED OFFICERS AND SOLDIERS LIKE YOU IN MY ARMY. BEHOLD — THE TEMPLE OF SOBK.

THE TEMPLE OF SOBK WAS LIKE MANY OTHER EGYPTIAN REMAINS OF ANTIQUITY — HIDDEN UNDER THE DRIFTING SAND FOR CENTURIES, WAITING ONLY TO BE FOUND. BUT THERE THE RESEMBLANCE ENDED.

THESE ARE MY TECHNICIANS. ITALIANS, GERMANS, SOUTH AFRICANS. IN ALL ARMIES THERE ARE MISFITS, DESERTERS, SOLDIERS OF FORTUNE. THESE I HAVE RECRUITED. BUT NOW, I NEED LEADERS.

THE MAD SHEIK'S PLAN WAS TO WAIT UNTIL THE EUROPEAN ARMIES HAD BECOME WEAKENED THROUGH FIGHTING ONE ANOTHER, THEN ATTACK AND DESTROY THE SURVIVORS. THUS HE WOULD DRIVE THE INFIDELS FROM HIS LAND AS HIS ANCESTOR HAD TRIED TO DO, SO MANY YEARS BEFORE.

BACK AT THE HOUSE, THE NEW MAHDI PUT A PROPOSITION TO THE THREE MEN.

YOU SEE MY POWER, MY WEAPONS. JOIN ME, AND I WILL MAKE YOU GENERALS. YOU WILL BE RICH MEN.

BRUNNER WAS THE FIRST TO REPLY. HE SPAT AT THE DERVISH LEADER'S FEET.

PAH! THAT IS WHAT I THINK OF YOUR POWER. THE AFRIKA KORPS WILL CRUSH YOU LIKE A BEETLE UNDER THEIR PANZERS.

COLONEL MICCA WAS MORE POLITE, BUT HIS ANSWER WAS THE SAME.

SHEIK HASSAN AHMED, YOU MADE A PACT WITH MY COUNTRY, AND NOW YOU BREAK IT. I REFUSE TO ASSIST YOU TO DO SO.

DAVE WILSON WAS BLUNT AND TO THE POINT.

YOU DON'T REALLY THINK THIS IDIOT IDEA HAS A HOPE? PACK IT IN BEFORE YOU GET HURT!

AGAIN THE WHIP CRACKED, AS THE VENEER OF EDUCATION SLIPPED FROM THE SELF-STYLED MAHDI. HE WAS ONCE AGAIN A SAVAGE ARAB.

INSOLENT DOG! NOW ALL THREE OF YOU WILL LEARN WHY I AM JUSTLY FEARED.

YOU HEAP OF CAMEL-FODDER! I'LL TEAR YOU APART FOR THAT.

WELL SAID, ENGLANDER!

THE SHEIK SEEMED TO GO COMPLETELY MAD. SCREAMING TORRENTS OF ABUSE, HE ORDERED THEM TO BE TIED UP.

INFIDEL DOGS! I WILL TEACH YOU TO SCORN ME! YOU SHALL BEG ME FOR MERCY. OTHERS HAVE MOCKED ME AND PAID DEARLY.

DAVE MENTIONED THE TWO TATTOOED AUSSIES. THE SHEIK WAS PLEASED TO EXPLAIN.

THOSE FOOLS! THEY LOST THEIR WAY IN A TRUCK AND CAME HERE. I OFFERED THEM TERMS, BUT THEY LAUGHED AT ME. THE HOLY MARK WAS TATTOOED BETWEEN THEIR EYES AND THEY WERE CAST INTO THE DESERT — TO LEARN REPENTANCE IN SLOW DEATH! NOW IT IS YOUR TURN — BRING THEM FORTH FOR THE FIRST ORDEAL!

THE SUN CLIMBED THE SKY, AND THE RAW STRIPS OF HIDE CLAMPED TIGHTER AND TIGHTER ON THEIR TAUT WRISTS, TILL THEY BECAME LIKE HOOPS OF RED-HOT STEEL...

MY WRISTS — THE PAIN —

SAVE YOUR BREATH, YOU'LL NEED IT ALL!

HOUR AFTER HOUR THE SCORCHING SUN BEAT DOWN UNTIL THE TORTURE BECAME UNBEARABLE. EACH MAN PRAYED FOR UNCONSCIOUSNESS TO COME BEFORE MADNESS. DAVE AND BRUNNER WERE SILENT, BUT MICCA WAS BEGINNING TO CRACK.

WATER! I BEG OF YOU — WATER!

SENSING THAT THE ITALIAN WAS WEAKEST, HASSAN PLAYED ON IT.

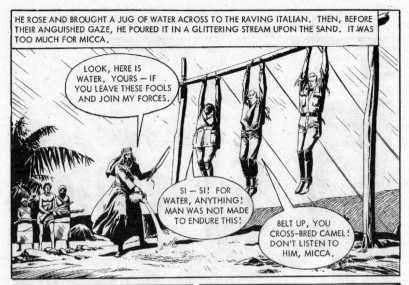

HE ROSE AND BROUGHT A JUG OF WATER ACROSS TO THE RAVING ITALIAN. THEN, BEFORE THEIR ANGUISHED GAZE, HE POURED IT IN A GLITTERING STREAM UPON THE SAND. IT WAS TOO MUCH FOR MICCA.

LOOK, HERE IS WATER. YOURS — IF YOU LEAVE THESE FOOLS AND JOIN MY FORCES.

SI — SI! FOR WATER, ANYTHING! MAN WAS NOT MADE TO ENDURE THIS!

BELT UP, YOU CROSS-BRED CAMEL! DON'T LISTEN TO HIM, MICCA.

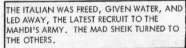

THE ITALIAN WAS FREED, GIVEN WATER, AND LED AWAY, THE LATEST RECRUIT TO THE MAHDI'S ARMY. THE MAD SHEIK TURNED TO THE OTHERS.

THE ITALIAN IS WISE. YOU TOO, WILL GIVE IN SOON.

NEVER! THE HONOUR OF THE REICH IS AT STAKE.

HASSAN AHMED SCREAMED IN RAGE AND DISAPPOINTMENT.

INFIDELS! YOU WILL LEARN TO OBEY ME! I HOLD YOUR LIVES IN THE PALM OF MY HAND. BUT WE WILL NOW TRY OTHER METHODS.

THEY WERE RELEASED AND DRAGGED, HALF-FAINTING, BACK INTO THE MAIN SQUARE OF THE OASIS.

THERE THE ARABS WERE LINED UP, GRINNING EVILLY AT THE THOUGHT OF THE TREAT IN STORE FOR THEM, BRANDISHING A WEIRD ASSORTMENT OF WEAPONS.

YOU STILL REFUSE TO JOIN ME? VERY WELL. YOU WILL NOW RUN THE GAUNTLET OF TERROR.

DROP DEAD!

WHEN THE AFRIKA KORPS TAKE EGYPT YOU WILL BE HANGED LIKE THE CRIMINAL YOU ARE.

THEY WERE PUSHED FORWARD TO RUN BETWEEN THE LINES OF WARRIORS, TO ENDURE THE PAIN OF A THOUSAND BLOWS.

EACH WARRIOR INFLICTED THE MAXIMUM SUFFERING WITHOUT ACTUALLY STUNNING THE VICTIMS. DAVE HAD TO GRIT HIS TEETH TO STOP HIMSELF YELLING WITH PAIN.

THEY STUMBLED THROUGH THE MOB IN AGONISED SILENCE, TO COLLAPSE IN THE DUST, BATTERED, BRUISED — BUT UNBROKEN.

THE SHEIK SCREAMED, HIS PATIENCE AT AN END. HE ORDERED THEM TO BE REVIVED. EVEN BRUNNER'S IRON WILL HAD BEEN SHAKEN BY THE ORDEAL, BUT NOT DAVE'S.

OBSTINATE FOOLS! ENOUGH OF THIS. NOW YOU COME TO TERMS OR DIE. BRING THEM OVER HERE!

NEIN — NO MORE...

THE SHEIK HAD A TALENT FOR FIENDISH DEVICES. THEY WERE MADE TO STAND FACING SHARP BAYONETS IN A RING OF WARRIORS. WEAK AS THEY WERE FROM THEIR ORDEAL, THEY WOULD HAVE TO STAND THERE AS LONG AS THE SHEIK WISHED. TO STUMBLE OR COLLAPSE MEANT CERTAIN DEATH.

HE COULD SHOW THE GESTAPO A THING OR TWO. WELL, I'M NOT FINISHED YET...NOT QUITE...

I DON'T THINK EITHER OF US CAN LAST MUCH LONGER.

SILENCE, DOG!

THE PITILESS SUN BEAT DOWN ON THE TWO MEN AS THEY STOOD AMID THE RING OF STEEL. EVERY MUSCLE ACHED FROM THE BEATING THEY HAD RECEIVED. BRUNNER SWAYED DANGEROUSLY, HIS ENDURANCE NEARLY AT AN END.

AACH! I — I SUBMIT!

HE WAS LED AWAY, A BROKEN MAN. AND STILL DAVE STOOD THERE, HIS INBRED TOUGHNESS GIVING HIM A GRIP OF IRON.

WELL, SERGEANT, HAVE YOU LEARNED SENSE YET?

I DON'T TAKE ORDERS FROM PIGS LIKE YOU.

THE SHEIK'S EYES FLAMED. HE GRABBED A RIFLE AND BAYONET. BUT DAVE WILSON WASN'T KEEN ON DYING — SLOWLY OR QUICKLY.

NOW THE FINISH — UGH!

BUT THEY WERE FAR TOO MANY, EVEN FOR A FIGHTER LIKE DAVE WILSON. HOURS LATER, HE CAME TO IN A FILTHY CELL.

ENGLISHMAN, YOU ARE EITHER VERY BRAVE OR FAVOURED BY ALLAH. I WILL NOW SEND YOU TO DIE SLOWLY IN THE DESERT — WITH THE MARK OF THE MAHDI ON YOUR FOREHEAD FOR ALL TO SEE.

DON'T COUNT ON IT, FRIEND.

YOU BOAST YOU ARE TOO TOUGH TO KILL. THEN THAT SHALL BE YOUR EPITAPH.

THE SHEIK CLAPPED HIS HANDS, AND A HUGE MAN ENTERED.

HERE IS SULIMAN. HE HAS A DELICATE TOUCH WITH THE THORNS AND INKS. SULIMAN WILL TATTOO YOU AN EPITAPH TO BE PROUD OF!

GRITTING HIS TEETH, DAVE MADE NO SOUND, THOUGH EACH PRICK OF THE THORN WAS AGONISING.

TOO TOUGH

FINALLY, THE EVIL WORK WAS DONE. THE MAD SHEIK SNIGGERED IN TRIUMPH.

"TOO TOUGH TO KILL". IT IS GOOD — THOUGH THOSE WHO FIND YOUR DEAD BODY WILL FIND IT IRONIC.

TOO TOUGH TO KILL

I'M NOT DEAD YET. I'LL BE BACK, JUST TO WRING YOUR SCRAWNY NECK. WE'LL SEE WHO LAUGHS LAST.

THE MAHDI HAD ONE MORE BOAST TO MAKE BEFORE CASTING DAVE OUT INTO THE DESERT. HE HAD HIM BROUGHT TO HIS HOUSE, INTO A SORT OF TROPHY ROOM...

SEE THIS FLAG, ENGLISHMAN. IT WAS CAPTURED FROM THE BRITISH WHEN WE CRUSHED THEM MANY YEARS AGO. IT WAS THE FIRST OF OUR TROPHIES, BUT IT WILL NOT BE THE LAST!

DAVE GASPED WHEN HE SAW IT WAS THE COLOUR OF HIS GRANDFATHER'S REGIMENT. A SCORE OF TIMES HE HAD HEARD THE STORY OF ITS LOSS FROM THE OLD MAN.

THAT NIGHT THEY TOOK SERGEANT DAVID WILSON FAR INTO THE DESERT AND LEFT HIM THERE, WITHOUT FOOD OR WATER. BUT HE DIDN'T LIE DOWN TO DIE. GUIDED BY THE STARS, HE PLODDED NORTH ALL NIGHT AND INTO THE SEARING HEAT OF THE DAY, TRYING TO KEEP HIS THOUGHTS BUSY SO THAT HE WOULD NOT GO MAD.

IMAGINE THAT COOT HAVING THE OLD REGIMENT'S FLAG ALL THESE YEARS. IF ONLY I COULD GET OUT OF THIS AND FETCH IT BACK. SOME HOPE...

FOR HOUR AFTER AGONISING HOUR, HE STRUGGLED ON.

MUST... GO...ON...

HE STAGGERED ON UNTIL THE WHITE FIERY BALL OF THE SUN SEEMED TO ENTER HIS BRAIN AND EXPLODE. AT LAST HIS LEGS BUCKLED.

WATER!

HE WOULD HAVE DIED THERE IF NOMADIC ARABS HADN'T FOUND HIM. EVEN THEN, HE'D HAVE DIED BUT FOR THE TATTOO. BEDOUINS WASTED NO SYMPATHY — OR WATER — ON ANY LOST SOLDIERS. BUT THE TATTOO IMPRESSED THEM.

IT IS A STRANGE SIGN. HE MAY BE A HOLY MAN. BRING HIM TO THE CAMP.

FOR FOUR DAYS HE WAS SHELTERED IN THE DESERT TENTS. ON THE FIFTH, A BEDOUIN SCOUT MET A PATROL LED BY JACK CAMERON, AND BROUGHT THEM TO THE TENT OF THE TATTOOED WHITE MAN.

SERGEANT WILSON! IT IS YOU — ISN'T IT?

IT'S ME ALL RIGHT, SKIPPER. A BIT WORSE FOR WEAR, BUT STILL IN ONE PIECE. I NEVER THOUGHT I'D LAY EYES ON YOU AGAIN.

AT FIRST THEY COULDN'T BELIEVE HIS INCREDIBLE STORY. THEY THOUGHT THE SUN HAD TOUCHED HIS BRAIN — UNTIL HE PULLED OFF HIS HEAD-DRESS.

YOU'VE GOT TO BELIEVE ME! LOOK — THIS IS WHAT THEY DID TO ME!

GOOD GRIEF! I GUESS THE MADMAN WHO DID THAT WOULD BE CAPABLE OF ANYTHING. STILL, HE WON'T FORGET US IN A HURRY WHEN WE'RE FINISHED WITH HIM.

DAVE HAD A BIT OF TROUBLE PREVENTING JACK FROM ATTACKING EL SUQ WITH TWO JEEPS. JACK HAD EVEN MORE DIFFICULTY WHEN HE REQUESTED THE SUPPORT OF A SQUADRON OF TANKS FROM HIS BRIGADIER.

I TELL YOU, SIR, THE PLACE IS A FORTRESS. I'LL NEED A SQUADRON OF TANKS AT LEAST. YES, I'VE ABSOLUTE FAITH IN MY SERGEANT'S REPORT.

IN TURN, THE BRIGADIER HAD TO PERSUADE A GENERAL THAT HE WAS NOT CRAZY. BUT FINALLY, A DAY LATER —

THEY WERE STILL SOME DISTANCE AWAY WHEN THE ARABS' ANTI-TANK GUNS OPENED UP.

SEE WHAT I MEAN? THEY'VE EVEN GOT ANTI-TANK GUNS. THESE GUYS CAN FIGHT AND NO MISTAKE, AND THEY'VE GOT THE STUFF TO DO IT WITH.

THE BATTLE OF EL SUQ WAS SHORT AND BITTER. THE MAHDI'S WARRIORS FOUGHT AS SAVAGELY AS THEIR ANCESTORS, BUT THE BRITISH HAD HEARD OF THEIR CRUELTY TO DAVE AND TO OTHER BRITISH SOLDIERS BEFORE HIM, AND THEY WERE OUT FOR BLOOD.

COME ON, I'LL TAKE YOU TO THEIR HIDDEN WORKSHOPS. THE TYPES WHO JOINED HASSAN'S PRIVATE ARMY WILL BE HIDING OUT THERE.

ON THE WAY TO THE TEMPLE OF SOBK, DAVE REMEMBERED HIS GRANDFATHER'S FLAG.

CARRY ON, I'VE SOMETHING TO COLLECT.

IN ABDUL'S HOUSE, DAVE WAS RECOVERING THE PRECIOUS COLOUR WHEN HE HEARD VOICES IN THE NEXT ROOM.

HASSAN! BETTER SEE WHAT HE'S UP TO.

TUCKING THE FLAG INSIDE HIS ROBES, DAVE EASED OPEN THE DOOR LEADING TO THE MAIN ROOM.

THE SELF-STYLED MAHDI AND TWO OF HIS WARRIORS WERE CARRYING BOXES OF HIGH-EXPLOSIVE DOWN THROUGH A TRAP-DOOR. HE SAW DAVE, BUT ONLY YELLED AT HIM IN ARABIC.

LAZY DOG! COME AND WORK!

HEY! HE THINKS I'M ONE OF HIS MOB. WONDER WHAT GOES ON? SEEMS HE WANTS ME TO LEND HIM A HAND.

HE PICKED UP A BOX AND FOLLOWED THE MEN INTO A GLOOMY TUNNEL BENEATH THE HOUSE.

THIS MUST HAVE BEEN PART OF THE TEMPLE WORKINGS AT ONE TIME.

THE PASSAGE CAME OUT IN THE JAWS OF THE HUGE TEMPLE IDOL. IN THE GREAT CHAMBER BELOW, THE BRITISH TANK CREWS WERE TAKING CHARGE OF THE PROCEEDINGS.

ALL RIGHT, YOU SHOWER, LINE UP OVER THERE AND WE'LL HAVE YOU OUT OF THIS FIRE-WORKS FACTORY OF YOURS SHARPISH.

THE SHEIK WAS MAKING A LAST DEFIANT GESTURE — HE HAD ENOUGH HIGH EXPLOSIVE TO BLOW UP THE IDOL, THE TEMPLE, AND ALL WITHIN.

WHEN THEY HAD SET DOWN THE EXPLOSIVES IN THE JAWS OF THE IDOL, THE SHEIK DISMISSED THE DERVISHES AND BEGAN TO SET FUSES EXPERTLY. BUT DAVE STAYED.

HIGHNESS — I HAVE SOMETHING TO SHOW YOU...

WHY DO YOU SPEAK IN ENGLISH? WHO ARE YOU?

DAVE SMILED GRIMLY AS HE PUSHED BACK HIS HOOD. THROUGH LONG HOURS OF AGONY HE HAD DREAMED OF THIS MOMENT.

THIS IS WHO I AM!

THE ENGLISHMAN!

RECOVERING FROM HIS SHOCK AND FEAR, THE MAD PROPHET FLASHED OUT HIS KNIFE AND SNARLED HIS DEFIANCE.

FOOL, YOU ARE UNARMED!

SO WHAT? I'LL KILL YOU WITH MY BARE HANDS.

FAST AS WAS THE MAHDI, DAVE WAS FASTER. A HAND LIKE A STEEL VICE CLAMPED ON THE ARAB'S THROAT.

TAKE A GOOD LOOK AT YOUR TATTOO, ARAB. IT'S THE LAST THING YOU'LL EVER SEE.

ON THE VERY EDGE OF THE IDOL'S JAWS THEY MATCHED STRENGTH — UNTIL, WITH A SUPER-HUMAN EXPLOSION OF ANGER AND HATRED, DAVE SWUNG THE EVIL MADMAN OFF HIS FEET, AND —

AAAAH!

AND THE FIRST HUMAN SACRIFICE FOR CENTURIES LAY SHATTERED BETWEEN THE STONE FEET OF THE TEMPLE IDOL, WHOSE BLIND EYES HAD GAZED ON LIFE AND DEATH FOR FOUR THOUSAND YEARS.

NUMB WITH REACTION, DAVE STAGGERED DOWN INTO THE MAIN HALL OF THE TEMPLE. THEY WATCHED HIM COME IN AWED SILENCE. MICCA AND BRUNNER WERE AMONG THE PRISONERS.

YOU DID WELL, ENGLANDER. THE DREAMS OF EL MAHDI ARE ENDED.

I, TOO, SALUTE YOUR COURAGE, SERGEANT.

COME ON, YOU TWO, YOU BIRDS CAN DO YOUR SINGING IN THE P.O.W. CAGE.

TAKE IT EASY WITH THOSE TWO, SARGE. WE'VE BEEN THROUGH A LOT TOGETHER.

SO ENDED THE MAHDI'S SECOND HOLY WAR. AGAIN A WILSON HAD FOUGHT — BUT THIS TIME THE FLAG OF THE FIGHTING 110th REGIMENT HAD BEEN WON BACK WITH HONOUR, AND SERGEANT DAVID WILSON REALLY HAD BEEN "TOO TOUGH TO KILL".

EQUIPMENT OF WWII

No.5 DAIMLER ARMOURED CAR

High mobility was the main feature of the Daimler Armoured Car. It could go backwards or forwards through all the gears at high speeds. Used mainly for reconnaissance duties, this vehicle could get out of trouble fast if it met any tanks — but it could also dish out plenty of trouble when it had to.

CREW —3
WEIGHT —7 tons
LENGTH —13ft
WIDTH —8ft
HEIGHT —7ft 4ins
SPEED —40mph

ENGINE —90hp Daimler
ARMAMENT — 2-pounder gun
Quick-firing 7.9mm machine gun
Bren gun can be mounted on turret rim
ARMOUR — 12mm (nearly half an inch) thick

FIGHTING FOOL!

LIEUTENANT BOB HENDERSON COMMANDED A
SPECIAL GROUP OF DESERT RAIDERS WHO HAD MADE
SWIFT ATTACKS BEHIND ENEMY LINES THEIR SPECIALITY.
SUCCESS DEPENDED UPON TEAMWORK, EACH MAN
KNOWING HE COULD RELY ON THE OTHERS.
BUT FOR TWO OF THE THREE NEW VOLUNTEERS
ARRIVING AT THE BASE, CO-OPERATION WAS
GOING TO BE VERY DIFFICULT . . .

THE NEWCOMERS, CORPORAL MIKE BRADDON AND PRIVATES JOE RUSSEL AND ANDY WRIGHT, WERE FRESH FROM THEIR SPECIAL OPERATIONS TRAINING AND THE LONG DRIVE TO THE CAMP IN THE BLISTERING DESERT SUN TIRED THEM OUT.

I'M GLAD THAT JOURNEY'S OVER, JOE. I COULD DO WITH A NICE COOL BEER AFTER THAT.

YOU'VE HAD THAT, THIS LOOKS LIKE THE RECEPTION COMMITTEE ON THE WAY.

JOE HAD JUST SPOTTED THEIR LIEUTENANT, BOB HENDERSON, APPROACHING, ACCOMPANIED BY HIS ABLE DEPUTY, SERGEANT GEORGE PHIPPS.

BOTH BOB AND GEORGE WERE SEASONED DESERT RAIDERS AND THEY MADE IT CLEAR WHAT THEY EXPECTED FROM THEIR NEW RECRUITS.

I KNOW THAT YOU HAVE SEEN PLENTY OF ACTION ALREADY. BUT YOU'RE GOING TO FIND THIS WORK A LOT DIFFERENT.

AND DON'T THINK YOU KNOW EVERYTHING JUST BECAUSE YOU'VE HAD SPECIAL TRAINING. FROM TOMORROW IT'LL BE THE REAL THING AND YOU'LL BE BEGINNERS ALL OVER AGAIN.

I CAN'T WAIT TO GET STARTED.

THE NEW MEN WERE REPLACEMENTS IN BOB'S UNIT AND HE WANTED THEM TO REALISE THAT THEY WERE PART OF A WELL-TRAINED FIGHTING UNIT.

YOU'RE PART OF A TEAM NOW, AND THAT MEANS YOU'VE GOT TO WORK TOGETHER. I ALSO WANT QUICK THINKING AND COMMON SENSE. UNDERSTAND?

GRIMLY THE THREE MEN NODDED.

AFTER GETTING HIS TOUGH SPEECH OUT OF THE WAY, BOB SPOKE TO EACH MAN IN TURN. THE FIRST THING HE NOTICED ABOUT MIKE WERE THE NEW CORPORAL'S STRIPES HE PROUDLY SPORTED ON HIS ARM.

I HOPE YOU'LL PROVE TO BE WORTHY OF THOSE TWO STRIPES, CORPORAL.

YOU CAN DEPEND ON ME, SIR.

MIKE WAS PROUD OF HIS PROMOTION AND WAS DETERMINED TO SHOW THAT HE HAD EARNED IT.

HIS ONLY PROBLEM WAS THAT JOE THOUGHT THAT HE WAS MUCH BETTER QUALIFIED TO BE A CORPORAL HAVING SEEN MORE ACTION, AND HE TOOK EVERY OPPORTUNITY TO VOICE HIS OPINION.

AT LEAST YOU AND I WILL BE ABLE TO SHOW THE LIEUTENANT WHAT GUTS ARE, ANDY.

MEANING I WON'T, RUSSEL? WELL WE'LL SEE ABOUT THAT BEFORE VERY MUCH LONGER.

BOB HAD ORDERED THE NEW MEN TO GET PLENTY OF REST AS THEY WERE TO MAKE AN EARLY START NEXT MORNING. BUT JOE SEEMED DETERMINED TO GIVE MIKE A SLEEPLESS NIGHT AS HE CONTINUED TO GOAD HIM.

I DIDN'T MEAN ANYTHING OUT THERE, CORPORAL. I-JUST FEEL HARD DONE BY, THAT'S ALL.

BECAUSE I GOT PROMOTION INSTEAD OF YOU NO DOUBT. WELL MAYBE YOU'VE GOT THE GUTS THIS LOT ARE LOOKING FOR—BUT NOT THE COMMON SENSE.

THAT REMARK REALLY STUNG JOE. HE WAS TOUGH AND NOT AFRAID TO TAKE RISKS, BUT IT HAD NOT GOT HIM ANYWHERE SO HE ROUNDED ANGRILY ON THE CORPORAL.

I'VE DONE MORE THAN ENOUGH IN THIS WAR TO EARN A PAIR OF STRIPES. WHAT HAVE YOU DONE THAT'S WORTH TALKING ABOUT?

WHY DON'T YOU ASK THE BLOKES WHO PROMOTED ME?

MIKE, ON THE OTHER HAND, WAS A QUIET TYPE AND LOOKED AS IF HE WOULDN'T HARM A FLY IF HE COULD HELP IT. BUT HE WAS SURE HE WAS UP TO THE CORPORAL'S JOB.

I'LL SHOW THAT LOUD-MOUTH THAT I'M THE MAN FOR THE JOB.

AT DAWN THE UNIT WAS BUSY PREPARING FOR THEIR LATEST RAID — A FUEL DUMP DEEP BEHIND ENEMY LINES.

PASS ME THOSE WATER CANS, WILL YOU?

RIGHT YOU ARE, MATE.

AFTER A FEW LAST MINUTE CHECKS, THE PARTY SET OFF IN TWO TRUCKS AND A JEEP. THEY WERE IN HIGH SPIRITS AND JOE MADE NO ATTEMPT TO HIDE HIS ENTHUSIASM.

ON OUR WAY AT LAST. I CAN'T WAIT TO GIVE THOSE JERRIES A HAMMERING.

THAT'S IF THEY DON'T GET US FIRST, MATE.

IT WAS OBVIOUS THAT MIKE, IN CHARGE OF THIS POWERFUL, WELL-ARMED CHEVROLET TRUCK, WAS TREATING THE MISSION MORE SERIOUSLY THAN HIS COMPANIONS.

THE DRIVE WAS FAR FROM LEISURELY. THEY HAD A LONG WAY TO GO AND BOB FORCED THE PACE UNTIL THEY WERE WELL INSIDE ENEMY TERRITORY.

NO SIGN OF ANY ENEMY ACTIVITY YET, SIR.

I HOPE IT STAYS THAT WAY, SERGEANT. WE CAN'T AFFORD ANY HOLD-UPS AT THIS STAGE.

BUT BOB WAS GOING TO HAVE HIS PLANS THWARTED. THE FIRST HOLD-UP TOOK THE FORM OF A BLOW-OUT IN THE FRONT TYRE OF MIKE'S TRUCK.

CRIKEY! WHAT'S HAPPENING?

NEVER MIND THAT. JUST HOLD TIGHT.

JOE, IN THE DRIVING SEAT, NEEDED ALL HIS SKILL TO CONTROL THE SKIDDING TRUCK AND BRING IT SAFELY TO A HALT.

THE FLAT TYRE MEANT AN UNSCHEDULED STOP AND A DELAY THAT BOB COULD WELL DO WITHOUT FOR IT WAS GETTING LATE AND HE WANTED TO SET UP CAMP BEFORE DARKNESS FELL.

OF ALL THE LUCK. YOU'D BETTER GET THAT WHEEL CHANGED QUICKLY, CORPORAL. I DON'T WANT TO HAVE TO USE LIGHTS AROUND HERE.

RIGHT, SIR.

THE RAIDERS TOOK EVASIVE ACTION AND BROKE FOR COVER IN SOME NEARBY ROCKS. THE ITALIANS WERE ABLE TO KEEP THEM PINNED DOWN EASILY. TO MAKE MATTERS WORSE, GEORGE PHIPPS HAD BEEN WOUNDED.

IT WAS PLAIN THAT THE BRITISH WERE IN A HOPELESS POSITION. BOB KNEW THAT ONLY ONE THING WAS LIKELY TO SAVE THEM FROM CERTAIN DEFEAT.

THE SOUND OF DISTANT FIGHTING WAS QUICKLY PICKED UP BY MIKE'S MEN AS THEY RACED TOWARD THE SCENE.

GET YOUR FOOT DOWN HARD, RUSSEL.

I DON'T NEED YOU TO TELL ME THAT.

AS THE TRUCK ROARED CLOSER HE COULD SEE WHO WAS TAKING THE POUNDING AND ALSO THAT THE ITALIANS WERE IN A STRONG POSITION.

STOP A MINUTE. I WANT TO GET A BETTER LOOK . . .

ARE YOU KIDDING? WHY DON'T WE JUST GET STUCK IN?

MIKE DID NOT NEED TO BE REMINDED ABOUT THE TROUBLE THE REST OF THE UNIT WERE IN. BUT HE CERTAINLY DIDN'T WANT TO FALL INTO THE SAME TRAP.

IF WE GO CHARGING IN LIKE A BULL AT A GATE WE COULD EASILY END UP IN THE SAME TIGHT SPOT. JUST DO AS YOU'RE TOLD FOR A CHANGE AND DON'T ARGUE.

THE ONLY ARGUMENT I WANT IS WITH THOSE ITALIANS.

ALTHOUGH HE DIDN'T WANT TO, JOE DECIDED HE'D BETTER DO WHAT HE WAS TOLD.

FROM A NEARBY VANTAGE POINT, MIKE COULD SEE THE ITALIAN SET-UP QUITE CLEARLY. HE DECIDED THERE AND THEN WHAT WAS NEEDED TO ROUT THEM.

I RECKON WE CAN GO STRAIGHT AT THEM AFTER ALL. THEY'RE TOO BUSY ATTACKING THE REST OF THE UNIT TO NOTICE US.

THIS IS CRAZY. THE FIGHT WILL BE OVER BEFORE WE CAN FIRE A SHOT IF IT'S LEFT TO BRADDON.

THE CORPORAL HAD BEEN GONE ONLY A MATTER OF MINUTES, BUT JOE, IMPATIENT AS EVER, COULDN'T WAIT TO ATTACK THE ENEMY AND RESCUE THE OTHERS.

HOLD TIGHT, LADS. WE'RE GOING IN.

HEY! WAIT FOR ME.

MIKE'S VOICE WAS DROWNED BY THE ROAR OF THE BIG ENGINE.

SEEING THE HAVOC JOE WAS CREATING UP ON THE HILL, THE BATTERED AMBUSH SURVIVORS CHARGED UP THE SLOPE TO ATTACK THE ITALIAN POSITIONS.

COME ON, MEN. NOW IT'S OUR TURN.

THE FIGHT FOR CONTROL OF THE HILL WAS BRIEF, WITH JOE'S GROUP EASILY COMING OUT ON TOP. VICTORY WAS MADE COMPLETE WHEN BOB'S MEN FINALLY CAME POURING INTO VIEW. THE REMAINING ITALIANS TURNED AND BEAT A HASTY RETREAT.

KEEP GOING, YOU LOT. ITALY'S JUST AROUND THE CORNER.

PHEW! ARE WE GLAD TO SEE YOU.

BOB WAS FULL OF PRAISE FOR THE ACTION THAT JOE HAD TAKEN. BUT HE WAS PUZZLED BY MIKE'S ABSENCE.

I EXPECTED TO SEE CORPORAL BRADDON IN CHARGE WHEN I ARRIVED.

HERE HE COMES NOW, SIR. LOOKS A BIT PUT OUT TO ME.

MIKE WAS PUT OUT ALL RIGHT. IN FACT HE WAS FURIOUS. JOE'S DISOBEDIENCE HAD MADE HIM LOOK COWARDLY AND STUPID.

YOU'RE A MANIAC, RUSSEL. WHY DIDN'T YOU WAIT FOR ME TO GET BACK TO YOU BEFORE RUSHING OFF LIKE THAT?

I DIDN'T THINK THERE WAS ENOUGH TIME LEFT FOR MR HENDERSON'S MEN, THAT'S WHY.

MIKE WAS NOT IMPRESSED BY JOE'S EXCUSE BUT BEFORE HE HAD A CHANCE TO TELL HIM SO, BOB STEPPED IN TO MEDIATE. THE WHOLE ARGUMENT WAS GETTING OUT OF HAND AND THE LIEUTENANT DIDN'T KNOW WHAT ALL THE FUSS WAS ABOUT.

JUST CALM DOWN, BOTH OF YOU, AND TELL ME WHAT ALL THIS IS ABOUT.

RUSSEL HERE DISOBEYED MY SPECIFIC ORDER, SIR.

IT WAS A SERIOUS ACCUSATION BUT BOB DEMANDED TO HEAR THE FULL STORY BEFORE COMING TO A DECISION.

THE WAY MIKE SAW IT, JOE'S ACTION COULD WELL HAVE LED TO DISASTER IF THE ITALIANS HAD BEEN BETTER EQUIPPED TO MEET THEM.

AND TO CROWN IT ALL, SIR, RUSSEL'S MADE ME LOOK AS IF I CAN'T DO MY JOB. I WANT HIM PUT UNDER OPEN ARREST.

THERE'S NO NEED TO GO THAT FAR, CORPORAL. WE'LL OVERLOOK IT THIS TIME. AFTER ALL, RUSSEL DID A GOOD JOB.

HAVING THROWN MIKE'S REQUEST OUT, BOB ORDERED JOE TO GO BACK TO THE TRUCK. HE WANTED A PRIVATE WORD WITH HIS CORPORAL AND HE MEANT BUSINESS.

RUSSEL SHOWED GUTS AND INITIATIVE JUST NOW. YOU CAN'T EXPECT ME TO ARREST A MAN FOR THAT.

I SUPPOSE NOT, SIR. BUT HE'S BEEN A THORN IN MY SIDE SINCE I WAS PROMOTED.

BOB MADE IT CLEAR THAT HE WAS NOT INTERESTED IN PERSONAL DIFFERENCES. IT WAS THE WAY THEY BEHAVED IN ACTION THAT MATTERED.

THIS WORK CALLS FOR QUICK THINKING, CORPORAL. REMEMBER THAT IF YOU WANT TO HOLD ON TO YOUR STRIPES.

I HAVEN'T MADE A VERY GOOD IMPRESSION SO FAR. AND IT'S ALL THANKS TO THAT HOT-HEAD RUSSEL.

THERE WAS NO TIME TO BROOD OVER THEIR MISFORTUNES HOWEVER, FOR THEY STILL HAD A LONG WAY TO GO BEFORE REACHING A SUITABLE CAMPING SITE.

THE RAIDERS PRESSED ON OVER A FAIR DISTANCE BEFORE SETTLING DOWN FOR THE NIGHT. WHEN THEY FINALLY DID, BOTH BOB AND GEORGE FOUND REST IMPOSSIBLE.

I COULDN'T SLEEP BECAUSE OF THE PAIN IN MY LEG, SIR. BUT WHAT'S TROUBLING YOU?

IT WAS EASY TO SEE THAT BOB HAD GOT SOMETHING ON HIS MIND. THE VETERAN SERGEANT WAS THE BEST MAN TO TALK TO ABOUT THE PROBLEM.

WHAT DO YOU THINK OF THE NEW BLOKES, RUSSEL AND BRADDON, SERGEANT. THEY DON'T SEEM TO GET ON TOO WELL AT ALL.

I'VE NOTICED, SIR. BUT I THINK THEY'VE BOTH GOT A LOT TO OFFER.

BOB WAS IMPRESSED WITH THE WAY JOE WORKED. IT WAS MIKE WHOM HE HAD DOUBTS ABOUT, THOUGH THE BATTLE-SEASONED SERGEANT DIDN'T SEEM TO SHARE THEM.

I SHOULDN'T WORRY TOO MUCH ABOUT THE CORPORAL, SIR. HE'S KEEN ENOUGH BUT HE WON'T TAKE STUPID RISKS. JUST GIVE HIM A CHANCE TO SHOW WHAT HE CAN DO.

HE HAD A CHANCE EARLIER AND HE MADE A MESS OF IT.

IN SPITE OF THE OUTCOME OF THE DAY'S EVENTS, GEORGE STILL HAD FAITH IN MIKE. HE TRIED TO PUT BOB'S FEARS TO REST.

I RECKON BRADDON HAD THE RIGHT IDEA TECHNICALLY, SIR. IN ANY CASE, I ALWAYS SAY THAT A MAN DOESN'T GET STRIPES IN THE BRITISH ARMY UNLESS THEY'VE BEEN EARNED.

THAT'S WHAT I'VE ALWAYS THOUGHT. BUT NOW I'M BEGINNING TO WONDER.

ON THE OTHER SIDE OF THE CAMP, MIKE WAS BROODING OVER HIS OWN PROBLEMS. TO HIS MIND, JOE AND ANDY WERE TWO OF THE BIGGEST HEADACHES HE HAD EVER HAD.

I RECKON YOU'VE ALREADY WON ONE OF THOSE STRIPES OFF BRADDON, JOE.

I KNOW. AND ONE MORE STUNT LIKE TODAY'S WILL GET ME THE SECOND. OLD MIKE MUST BE WORRIED SICK.

I OUGHT TO PULL THOSE TWO UP FOR MAKING REMARKS LIKE THAT. BUT I DOUBT IF I'D GET MR HENDERSON'S SUPPORT.

THE NEXT MORNING FOUND THE RAIDERS MAKING READY TO STRIKE CAMP. THEY WERE IN FOR A NASTY SHOCK HOWEVER AS JOE CHECKED THE WATER SUPPLY.

HEY! THERE'S NO WATER IN THIS CAN.

HOW DID THAT HAPPEN?

THE WATER CANS WERE RIDDLED WITH HOLES WHERE THEY HAD BEEN PIERCED BY MORTAR SHELL FRAGMENTS DURING THE PREVIOUS DAY'S FIGHTING.

THEY'VE BEEN PUNCTURED UNDERNEATH, SIR. THAT'S WHY WE DIDN'T NOTICE.

AND EVERY ONE THE SAME. WHAT ROTTEN LUCK.

WELL THEY CAN BE REPAIRED. BUT IT WILL MEAN A DETOUR TO FIND SOME MORE WATER, I'M AFRAID.

ONCE AGAIN TIME WAS PRESSING. BOB KNEW THAT THE NEAREST WATER-HOLE WAS SOME DISTANCE AWAY AND WOULD TAKE PRECIOUS TIME TO REACH.

BOB CONFIDED HIS WORRIES TO GEORGE.

IF THERE ARE ANY JERRIES AT THIS OASIS, IT MEANS ANOTHER FIGHT. THERE ISN'T ENOUGH TIME.

WELL, WHY NOT SEND BRADDON'S SECTION AHEAD TO SCOUT.

ALTHOUGH BOB WAS RELUCTANT, IT SEEMED LIKE THE BEST IDEA.

MIKE'S SECTION WAS READY TO LEAVE WITHIN MINUTES WITH A FEW INSTRUCTIONS FROM BOB TO HELP THEM ALONG.

HAVE A GOOD LOOK AROUND, AND DON'T FORGET —USE YOUR INITIATIVE.

I KNOW, MATE, AND QUICK THINKING AS WELL.

AFTER A COUPLE OF HOURS HARD DRIVING, THEY CAME TO SOME HILLY COUNTRY. THEY WERE GETTING CLOSE TO THEIR OBJECTIVE.

IT'S TIME WE LEFT THE ROAD. IF THERE ARE ANY JERRIES AT THAT WATER-HOLE WE WANT TO COME OUT WHERE THEY LAST EXPECT US.

WHATEVER YOU SAY, CORPORAL. YOU'RE IN CHARGE.

THERE WAS A HINT OF SARCASM IN JOE'S VOICE.

MIKE REALISED THAT HE AND JOE WERE HEADING FOR ANOTHER SHOWDOWN AND DECIDED TO CLEAR THE AIR THERE AND THEN. HE ASKED JOE WHAT WAS ON HIS MIND.

YOU KNOW WHAT THE LIEUTENANT SAID ABOUT SAVING TIME. IF WE LEAVE THE ROAD WE MIGHT GET STUCK IN THE SAND.

WELL, THAT'S BETTER THAN GETTING PINNED DOWN BY ENEMY GUNS BECAUSE WE CHARGED IN WITHOUT HAVING A LOOK FIRST.

IT WAS WELL KNOWN THAT WANDERING TRIBES WERE NOT TO BE TRUSTED.

I WONDER WHOSE SIDE THAT BUNCH ARE ON.

THERE'S ONLY ONE WAY TO FIND OUT.

HOW?

AS USUAL JOE STARTED TO OBJECT AS SOON AS MIKE OUTLINED HIS PLAN.

I'LL CREEP DOWN AND HAVE A LOOK AROUND. THERE'S SURE TO BE SOMETHING TO LET US KNOW WHOSE SIDE THEY'RE ON.

WHY WASTE TIME? LET'S GO IN FIGHTING AND HAVE DONE WITH IT.

JOE'S PLAN WAS SIMPLE ENOUGH BUT IMPRACTICAL AS MIKE WAS QUICK TO POINT OUT.

WHAT HAPPENS IF THEY'RE ON OUR SIDE, YOU IDIOT. SHOOTING THEM DOWN WILLY-NILLY WOULDN'T BE VERY GOOD FOR HELPING US WIN FRIENDS, WOULD IT?

ALL RIGHT THEN, HAVE IT YOUR OWN WAY.

LEAVING STRICT INSTRUCTIONS THAT NO ONE SHOULD FOLLOW HIM UNTIL BOB SHOWED UP, HE GRABBED HIS TOMMY GUN, AND SET OFF ON HIS DANGEROUS ONE-MAN MISSION.

HE'S JUST TRYING TO GET BACK INTO THE LIEUTENANT'S GOOD BOOKS, THAT'S ALL.

THERE HE GOES, ANDY. HUNTING FOR GLORY.

MIKE WAS ONLY INTERESTED IN FINDING OUT IF THE NOMADS WERE FRIENDLY OR NOT. HE WAS NOT INTERESTED IN BECOMING A HERO, NO MATTER WHAT THE REWARDS.

SO FAR SO GOOD. SINCE THAT TENT IS GUARDED I'LL TRY THERE FIRST.

HE HAD LITTLE DIFFICULTY IN CUTTING HIS WAY INTO THE TENT WHICH HE FOUND WAS UNOCCUPIED.

NOBODY ABOUT I SEE. WELL, THAT MAKES THINGS A LOT EASIER FOR ME.

WORKING SWIFTLY AND SILENTLY IN ORDER TO AVOID DISCOVERY, MIKE HAD SOON PRISED THE LID FROM ONE OF THE MANY CRATES WHICH WERE STACKED INSIDE THE TENT.

AH HA, THIS LOOKS INTERESTING.

THE BOX CONTAINED GLEAMING, BRAND-NEW ITALIAN RIFLES, AND THAT TOLD HIM EVERYTHING HE WANTED TO KNOW ABOUT THE ARABS' LOYALTIES.

CHRISTMAS PRESENTS FROM MUSSOLINI, NO DOUBT. WELL AT LEAST IT PROVES THAT THIS MOB AREN'T ON OUR SIDE.

WITH THE DISCOVERY THAT THE ARABS WERE PRO-AXIS, MIKE DECIDED TO LEAVE — QUICKLY.

AS USUAL, JOE BECAME IMPATIENT WITH ALL THE WAITING ABOUT. HE DECIDED TO DISREGARD MIKE'S ORDER ONCE MORE AND DO A BIT OF INVESTIGATING FOR HIMSELF.

HEY, JOE! WHERE ARE YOU GOING?

TO FIND OUT WHAT BRADDON'S PLAYING AT.

AS HE DREW CLOSE TO THE BEDOUIN ENCAMPMENT JOE WAS FORCED TO HIDE IN A DITCH TO AVOID AN ARAB GUARD. FROM HIS REFUGE HE NOTICED MIKE MERGING FROM THE TENT.

THERE HE IS NOW. BEEN HAVING FORTY WINKS I SHOULDN'T WONDER.

WHAT ON EARTH IS RUSSEL DOING HERE?

MIKE WAS PUZZLED, AND MORE THAN A LITTLE ANNOYED, TO FIND THAT THE REBELLIOUS PRIVATE HAD FOLLOWED HIM.

ALMOST IMMEDIATELY THE WHOLE CAMP WAS THROWN INTO CONFUSION. MIKE HELPED TO REPEL THE FIRST ONSLAUGHT THEN REALISED HE WAS SITTING IN A TIGHT SPOT HIMSELF.

THEY'LL BE COMING FOR THEIR GUNS IN A MOMENT AND THERE'S ONLY ME HERE TO STOP THEM.

SURE ENOUGH, AS SOON AS THE NOISE OF GUNFIRE DIED AWAY, A GROUP OF ARABS DASHED INTO THE TENT TO BREAK OUT NEW RIFLES. MIKE HOWEVER HAD SLIPPED BACK INSIDE AND WAS ON HAND TO GREET THEM.

GET BACK YOU SCUM!

AAAAGH!

UUUUGH!

ALTHOUGH HE HAD DEALT WITH THE FIRST ATTACK, HE KNEW THAT HE COULDN'T HOLD OUT FOR LONG NOW THAT THE ELEMENT OF SURPRISE WAS LOST, SO HE HURRIEDLY MOVED TO JOIN JOE.

THE MEN WHO HAD STAYED PUT ON THE RIDGE WERE ABLE TO GIVE LIMITED COVERING FIRE, BUT MIKE AND JOE WERE STILL IN A DIFFICULT POSITION.

JUST AS MIKE WAS BEGINNING TO GIVE UP HOPE, JOE LET OUT A GLEEFUL YELL — HE HAD SPOTTED BOB APPROACHING IN THE OTHER TRUCK.

AT BOB'S TIMELY ARRIVAL, THE ARABS DECIDED TO BEAT A HASTY RETREAT, LEAVING MIKE AND JOE RELIEVED AND UNSCATHED.

GET STUCK IN, LADS. RUN THEM DOWN.

AAAAAIEEEE! FLEE FOR YOUR LIVES.

AS THE DUST SETTLED THE MOOD QUICKLY CHANGED FROM ONE OF CO-OPERATION AS MIKE RUEFULLY REALISED HE HAD YET ANOTHER SCORE TO SETTLE WITH JOE.

YOU SHOWED UP IN THE NICK OF TIME, SIR.

YOU MANIAC, RUSSEL. YOUR DISOBEDIENCE ALMOST GOT US BOTH KILLED.

WHAT ARE YOU TALKING ABOUT, CORPORAL?

MIKE RECOUNTED THE EVENTS WHICH HAD LED TO THE GUN BATTLE.

AS USUAL, JOE HAD AN IMPRESSIVE EXCUSE FOR HIS ACTIONS.

YOU'D BEEN GONE SO LONG, CORPORAL. I JUST CAME DOWN TO SEE IF YOU'D HAD SOME TROUBLE.

THE ONLY TROUBLE I HAD WAS CAUSED BY YOU, RUSSEL. YOU SHOULD BE COURT-MARTIALLED FOR YOUR STUPIDITY.

AS THINGS WERE CLEARLY GETTING OUT OF HAND BETWEEN MIKE AND JOE, BOB FELT IT WAS NECESSARY TO COOL THINGS DOWN BEFORE THEY CAME TO BLOWS.

THE CORPORAL'S PERFECTLY RIGHT, RUSSEL. YOU SHOULDN'T HAVE DISOBEYED ORDERS AND FOLLOWED HIM. BUT, SINCE EVERYTHING WORKED OUT WELL IN THE END, I'M PREPARED TO OVERLOOK THE MATTER.

WHY, HE ALMOST GOT ME KILLED!

BOB DISMISSED JOE AND WAITED TILL HE WAS OUT OF EARSHOT BEFORE CONTINUING.

ALTHOUGH BOB UNDERSTOOD HOW MIKE MUST HAVE FELT, THERE WAS MUCH MORE THAN HIS FEELINGS AT STAKE.

JUST FORGET WHAT'S HAPPENED AND KNUCKLE DOWN TO THIS DICEY JOB!

WELL, I'LL BE BLOWED.

HE WAS RESENTFUL AT THE WAY THE NEAR FATAL INCIDENT WAS BEING TREATED.

IF HE PREFERS THAT HOT-HEAD'S METHODS TO MINE HE CAN HAVE THEM. AS SOON AS THIS MISSION'S OVER, I WANT A TRANSFER.

WITH THEIR WATER TANKS PATCHED UP AND REFILLED THEY WERE READY TO MOVE OFF ONCE MORE. JOE'S TRUCK, HOWEVER, WAS THE SCENE OF SOME EXCITED CHATTER.

THE CORPORAL'S HAD ENOUGH OF THIS LOT, JOE. IT'S WRITTEN ALL OVER HIS FACE.

THAT'D MEAN TWO STRIPES UP FOR GRABS — AND I KNOW WHO SHOULD GET THEM.

JOE WAS SURE HE WOULD GET PROMOTION IF MIKE LEFT THE UNIT.

THE UNIT DROVE HARD THROUGHOUT THE REST OF THE DAY AND BY LATE AFTERNOON THEY HAD MADE UP THE LOST TIME.

PULL OVER, MEN. WE'LL MAKE CAMP HERE.

THANK GOODNESS FOR THAT. I'M WHACKED.

BOB LED MIKE UP THE STEEP EMBANKMENT TO HAVE A LOOK AROUND AS HE WAS SURE THAT THE FUEL DUMP WAS NEARBY.

I HOPE THEY FIND WHAT THEY'RE LOOKING FOR.

DON'T WORRY. WE HAVEN'T MISSED A TARGET YET.

ON REACHING THE TOP OF THE DUNE, BOB AND MIKE WERE ABLE TO SEE THEIR OBJECTIVE QUITE CLEARLY. MIKE FELT A TWINGE OF EXCITEMENT RUN THROUGH HIM AT THE PROSPECT OF MORE ACTION.

HERE WE ARE, CORPORAL. JOURNEY'S END.

WE'RE ON SCHEDULE TOO, SIR. IN SPITE OF ALL THE HOLD-UPS.

THERE WAS PLENTY OF ACTIVITY AT THE DUMP WITH ENEMY CONVOYS COMING AND GOING. BUT IT WAS STILL DAYLIGHT AND BOB HOPED FOR A FALL OFF IN TRAFFIC BEFORE DARKNESS FELL.

WE'VE GOT ENOUGH TIME BEFORE WE GO IN ANYWAY. IT SHOULD QUIETEN DOWN BY THE TIME WE HAVE TO MOVE.

I HOPE SO, SIR. WE DON'T WANT TO HAVE TO GO DODGING TRAFFIC, DO WE?

MIKE MADE NO SECRET OF THE FACT THAT HE WAS KEEN TO GET ON WITH THE JOB. FOR THAT REASON BOB DECIDED IT WAS TIME THAT THE CORPORAL KNEW THAT HE WOULDN'T BE TAKING PART IN THE RAID ITSELF.

I'VE ALREADY DECIDED ON THE MEN FOR THE ASSAULT TEAM, CORPORAL. I HOPE YOU DON'T TAKE IT TOO HARD BUT I'D LIKE YOU TO REMAIN HERE.

BUT, SIR. WHY ARE YOU LEAVING ME OUT?

MIKE WAS BITTERLY DISAPPOINTED WITH BOB'S DECISION AND HE DIDN'T HAVE TO STRETCH HIS IMAGINATION TO KNOW WHY BOB DIDN'T WANT HIM ALONG.

IT DID NOT TAKE LONG FOR NEWS TO GET AROUND THE REST OF THE UNIT. ALTHOUGH GEORGE FELT SYMPATHETIC TOWARDS THE CORPORAL, THAT COULD HARDLY BE SAID ABOUT JOE AND ANDY.

DID YOU HEAR THAT, ANDY? THE LIEUTENANT DOESN'T WANT BRADDON.

HE MUST THINK HE'S NOT UP TO THE JOB. I CAN'T SAY I'M SURPRISED.

AS DARKNESS FELL, THE GROUP WHO WERE TO MAKE THE ATTACK WERE CHECKING THEIR EQUIPMENT. ONCE THEY GOT MOVING THERE COULD BE NO TURNING BACK. EVERYONE WAS INVOLVED EXCEPT GEORGE, MIKE AND PRIVATE LEN HARVEY, THE WIRELESS OPERATOR.

RIGHT, EVERYONE DOUBLE-CHECK THEIR KIT. I WANT TO SEE SOME FIREWORKS TONIGHT.

WHEN BOB MOVED NEARER, IT QUICKLY BECAME OBVIOUS THERE WERE NO GUARDS PRESENT. THE GERMANS HAD PLANTED A MINE-FIELD AT THE VERY PLACE THE MEN HAD INTENTED TO CUT THE FENCE.

ACHTUNG! MINEN

THAT'S ALL WE NEED. LOOKS LIKE A JOB FOR A STEADY HAND.

BOB WENT BACK TO THE MAIN GROUP AND RETURNED WITH HIS LANCE-CORPORAL WHO HAD VOLUNTEERED TO HELP HIM CLEAR A PATH. THE WORK WAS AGONISINGLY SLOW AND TREACHEROUS.

HERE'S ANOTHER ONE. SO MIND WHERE YOU'RE WALKING.

DON'T WORRY ABOUT THAT, SIR. I'M ON TIPTOES NOW.

CLEARING MINES WAS A NERVE-WRACKING BUSINESS BUT WATCHING AND WAITING WAS NOT EASY EITHER, ESPECIALLY FOR JOE AND ANDY.

I WISH THEY COULD GET A MOVE ON. ALL THIS HANGING ABOUT GIVES ME THE JITTERS.

I KNOW HOW YOU FEEL, MATE.

AT LAST THE WAITING WAS OVER AND THE MEN EAGERLY GOT ON THE MOVE AGAIN.

GO DOWN TO THE ROAD ONE AT A TIME. FOLLOW THE TRAIL THROUGH THE MINES TO THE FENCE.

RIGHT, CORP. WE'RE ON OUR WAY.

THE HOLD-UP HAD MADE ANDY FEEL UNEASY. THE PROSPECT OF TACKLING THE MINE-FIELD DID NOT HELP HIS NERVES.

THERE'S NO COVER ACROSS THAT ROAD. IF ANY JERRIES PASS BY I'LL REALLY BE IN THE SOUP.

BUT THERE WAS TO BE NO TURNING BACK. HE HAD TO PRESS ON.

JOE WAS FOLLOWING CLOSE BEHIND ANDY BUT HE DIDN'T FEEL ANY BETTER. HE WAS A MAN OF ACTION WHO WORKED ON IMPULSE. HE TOO HAD BEEN UNNERVED BY TOO MUCH WATCHING AND WAITING.

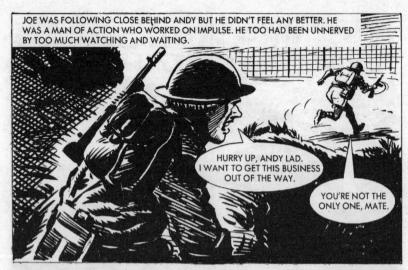

HURRY UP, ANDY LAD. I WANT TO GET THIS BUSINESS OUT OF THE WAY.

YOU'RE NOT THE ONLY ONE, MATE.

ANDY WAS ABOUT HALFWAY THROUGH THE MINE-FIELD WHEN A GERMAN PATROL APPEARED. IT WAS THEN THAT THE HAPLESS PRIVATE REALLY STARTED TO PANIC.

BLIMEY! I'VE HAD IT NOW.

JUST KEEP YOUR HEAD DOWN, WRIGHT AND EVERYTHING WILL BE FINE.

IT DIDN'T HELP MATTERS WHEN A SPOTLIGHT MOUNTED ON THE ENEMY TRUCK BEGAN SWEEPING OVER THE AREA WHERE ANDY WAS LYING.

THEY'LL SPOT ME FOR SURE IF I STAY HERE. I'M GOING FOR THE WIRE.

HE STOOD UP AND STARTED TO RUN.

HIS DASH FOR SAFETY HAD DISASTROUS CONSEQUENCES. THE GERMANS QUICKLY PICKED HIM OUT OF THE DARKNESS.

ACHTUNG! MAN IN THE MINE-FIELD.

OPEN FIRE.

AAAAAAAGH!

ANDY DIED IN A MURDEROUS HAIL OF GERMAN BULLETS.

BECAUSE OF HIS BROKEN NERVE, HIS AIM WAS WELL OFF THE MARK. HE WATCHED AS HIS GRENADE EXPLODED HARMLESSLY AT THE SIDE OF THE TRUCK AND WHEN MORE GERMANS ARRIVED ON THE SCENE HE TURNED AND FLED.

THAT'S AS MUCH AS I CAN DO. IT'S EVERY MAN FOR HIMSELF NOW.

IN A BLIND PANIC, THE PRIVATE HEADED STRAIGHT BACK TOWARDS THE CAMP.

BOB AND THE OTHERS PUT UP A BRAVE FIGHT. BUT WITH THE ARRIVAL OF GERMAN REINFORCEMENTS THE LIEUTENANT COULD SEE THAT FURTHER RESISTANCE WAS FUTILE.

WELL, THAT'S THE END OF THE AMMO, LADS. I THINK IT'S TIME TO CHUCK IN THE TOWEL.

RIGHT, SIR. I'LL PASS THE WORD.

THE SURVIVORS WERE QUICKLY ROUNDED UP AND SEARCHED. WHEN THE GERMAN COMMANDING OFFICER WAS SATISFIED THEY WERE SAFE HE HAD THEM LED AWAY TO THE GUARD-HOUSE.

WATCH THEM CAREFULLY. IF THEY TRY ANY TRICKS —SHOOT THEM!

WHAT A DISASTER.

BACK AT THE TRUCKS THEY COULD HEAR THE FIGHTING. THEY KNEW THAT THERE HAD BEEN TROUBLE.

THE SHOOTING HAS STOPPED.

MAYBE I SHOULD GO AND INVESTIGATE.

LET'S JUST WAIT AND SEE WHAT HAPPENS.

THEY DID NOT HAVE TO WAIT LONG. JOE WAS SOON BACK AT THE CAMP BUT HE WAS IN A TERRIBLE STATE.

IT'S RUSSEL. HE LOOKS WORN OUT.

GET THE TRUCKS STARTED. WE'VE GOT TO CLEAR OUT.

HE RUSHED TO HIS TRUCK WITHOUT ANOTHER WORD. MIKE COULD SEE THE PANIC
IN HIS EYES AND TRIED TO CALM HIM DOWN TO GET THE DETAILS.

HOLD YOUR
HORSES, JOE. TELL US
WHAT'S HAPPENED.

I'LL TELL YOU LATER,
WE'VE GOT TO GET
OUT OF THIS PLACE!

JOE DECIDED TO BE AWKWARD SINCE MIKE WOULDN'T LET HIM
GO. THE TOUGH PRIVATE STRUCK OUT WITH HIS FIST BUT MIKE
WAS READY FOR HIM AND DELIVERED A JAW-NUMBING PUNCH
OF HIS OWN.

YOU'RE NOT
GOING ANYWHERE
YET, YOU BIG APE!

URGH!

MIKE CALMLY POINTED OUT THAT THEY STILL HAD PLENTY OF EXPLOSIVE CHARGES AND IT WOULD BE SIMPLE FOR HIMSELF AND JOE TO RETURN IMMEDIATELY AND LAY THEM.

THE JERRIES WON'T BE EXPECTING ANOTHER ATTACK TONIGHT. WE'LL HAVE SURPRISE ON OUR SIDE FOR SURE.

THAT'S TRUE. BUT HOW DOES RUSSELL FEEL ABOUT LEADING YOU BACK THERE?

GEORGE COULD SEE THAT JOE WAS NEAR TO BREAKING POINT AND MIGHT GO TO PIECES AND CAUSE ANOTHER DISASTER.

I'M NOT SURE I CAN GO BACK THERE. NOT SO SOON ANYWAY.

COME ON, JOE. I THOUGHT THAT YOU WERE MADE OF STERNER STUFF THAN THIS.

MIKE HOPED THAT HE COULD RE-AWAKEN JOE'S PRIDE IN HIMSELF SO THAT HE WOULD AGREE TO LEAD HIM TO THE DUMP.

JOE LED MIKE ALONG THE ROUTE TO THE DUMP. WHEN THEY ARRIVED HOWEVER THEY DISCOVERED TWO NEW OBSTACLES IN THEIR WAY. MIKE WAS NOT TOO DISTURBED BY THE PRESENCE OF THE GUARDS.

THEY'RE NOT EXPECTING TROUBLE. THEY LOOK HALF ASLEEP.

JOE WAS BEGINNING TO FEEL THAT HE HAD UNDER-ESTIMATED THE COOL, CALCULATING CORPORAL.

THE GERMAN GUARDS PAID DEARLY FOR THEIR SLACKNESS AS THE TWO RAIDERS SLIPPED UNSEEN FROM THE SHADOWS, THEIR KNIVES POISED FOR ACTION.

URGH!

GOODNIGHT, FRITZ.

QUICKLY THEY BUNDLED THE TWO DEAD GERMANS INTO THE DITCH AT THE SIDE OF THE ROAD.

AS MIKE HAD EXPECTED, THE PATH THROUGH THE MINE-FIELD WAS STILL CLEAR AND THE DUO WERE ABLE TO ENTER THE FUEL DUMP WITHOUT ANY TROUBLE. MIKE WAS GLAD TO SEE THAT THE ACTIVITY HAD CALMED JOE DOWN.

STILL NERVOUS, JOE?

JUST KEEP ME BUSY AND I'LL BE FINE.

ONCE INSIDE THE COMPOUND, MIKE MADE FOR THE LARGEST STACK OF FUEL AND SET JOE TO WORK WITH THE EXPLOSIVE CHARGES.

ANY ONE ABOUT, CORPORAL?

LET ME WORRY ABOUT THAT.

MORE THAN ONCE THE TWO RAIDERS CAME DANGEROUSLY CLOSE TO BEING DISCOVERED. IT TOOK A COOL HEAD NOT TO START A SHOOT-OUT.

QUIET, JOE.

WHY? WHAT'S WRONG?

EVERYTHING NOW DEPENDED ON GEORGE IF THE RESCUE PLAN WAS TO SUCCEED. BUT FIRST MIKE AND JOE HAD TO FIND OUT WHERE THE CAPTIVES WERE BEING HELD.

THAT HUT OVER THERE IS THE ONLY ONE THAT'S GUARDED. I'LL BET THAT'S WHERE OUR LADS ARE.

YOU'D THINK HE WAS OUT FOR A MORNING STROLL FOR ALL THE NERVES HE'S SHOWING.

WHILE THEY WERE PREPARING TO RELEASE THEIR COMRADES, GEORGE WAS ORGANISING HIS PART OF THE PROCEEDINGS.

THEY'LL HAVE LAID THE CHARGES BY NOW, SO WE'D BETTER BE ON OUR WAY.

I'M RIGHT BEHIND YOU, SARGE.

IN SPITE OF THE PAIN IN HIS LEG, GEORGE WAS EAGER TO GET GOING. HE THUMBED THE TRUCK'S STARTER AND SET OFF FOR THE SLOPE ABOVE THE MINE-FIELD.

HE HAD ONLY JUST GOT THEIR TRUCK MOVING WHEN THERE WAS A DEAFENING ROAR AS THE OTHER CHEVROLET HIT A MINE AND EXPLODED IN FLAMES. IT WAS ALL PART OF THE PLAN.

THERE SHE BLOWS.

SO FAR SO GOOD, ANYWAY, SARGE.

WITHIN SECONDS THE WHOLE GERMAN FORCE WAS MAKING ITS WAY TOWARDS THE SCENE OF THE EXPLOSION. THEY WERE AFRAID THE FIRE MIGHT SPREAD TO THE MOUNTAINS OF HIGHLY INFLAMMABLE FUEL.

HIMMEL! HERE WE GO AGAIN.

SCHNELL! MAN THE FIRE-TENDER.

AS THE CLAMOUR TO PUT THE DISTANT FIRE OUT HAD LEFT THE AREA AROUND THEIR OBJECTIVE PRETTY WELL DESERTED, THE TWO RAIDERS REACHED THE GUARD-HOUSE UNOBSERVED.

BETTER GO QUIETLY. THERE MAY BE MORE GUARDS INSIDE.

I CAN HANDLE THESE TWO MYSELF.

AS JOE CRACKED THE GERMANS' HEADS TOGETHER, MIKE KICKED OPEN THE DOOR OF THE HUT. HE WAS FULLY EXPECTING A SHOOT OUT.

SWEET DREAMS, YOU TWO.

HERE GOES.

THE RAIDERS DID NOT WASTE ANY TIME TAKING OVER THE GERMAN VEHICLE.
JOE WAS THE LAST ABOARD.

LIBERATING THE PRISONERS HAD BEEN RELATIVELY EASY. MIKE REALISED GRIMLY THAT
GETTING OUT OF THE COMPOUND WAS GOING TO BE A DIFFERENT MATTER.

BOB DECIDED THAT THERE WAS ONLY ONE COURSE OF
ACTION THEY COULD TAKE.

AS MIKE HAD ANTICIPATED THE MEN AT THE MAIN GATE WERE ARMED TO THE TEETH. THEY ALSO SEEMED VERY MUCH MORE ALERT THAN THE PREVIOUS SENTRIES.

DRIVE UP SLOWLY, CORPORAL. WE DON'T WANT TO AROUSE THEIR SUSPICION TOO SOON.

I HOPE THIS WORKS.

THE RUSE MANAGED TO GET THEM TO THE GATE, BUT AS EXPECTED THE GUARD WANTED A CLOSER LOOK AT THE MEN IN THE HALF-TRACK.

HALT!

RIGHT, MEN. LET 'EM HAVE IT.

MIKE SLAMMED HIS FOOT DOWN HARD ON THE ACCELERATOR AS THE RAIDERS OPENED UP ON THE GERMANS.

THE FIRE FROM THE HALF-TRACK WAS DEADLY ACCURATE. THE GERMAN MACHINE GUNNERS STOOD NO CHANCE OF SURVIVAL IN THE DEVASTATING FUSILLADE.

WITH THE ENGINE SCREAMING, THE HALF-TRACK EXPLODED THROUGH THE GATES OF THE FUEL DUMP. THE GERMAN RESISTANCE WAS STIFF HOWEVER AND THE RAIDERS DID NOT ESCAPE UNSCATHED.

THE NEXT DAY FOUND THEM RESTING AT AN OASIS. THE BREAK GAVE JOE A CHANCE TO GET ONE OR TWO THINGS OFF HIS CHEST.

YOU WORKED WONDERS AT THE FUEL DUMP LAST NIGHT, CORPORAL. I RECKON THE RIGHT BLOKE'S BEEN WEARING THE STRIPES ALL THE TIME.

I JUST HOPE WE CAN WORK TOGETHER AS A TEAM FROM NOW ON, JOE.

MIKE WAS MORE THAN WILLING TO FORGIVE JOE'S PREVIOUS BEHAVIOUR BECAUSE HE WAS SURE THAT THE PRIVATE HAD LEARNT HIS LESSON.

JOE FELT THAT HE ALSO OWED BOB AN EXPLANATION.

I'M SORRY I RAN OUT ON YOU, SIR. I JUST DIDN'T KNOW WHAT ELSE TO DO.

FORGET IT, RUSSEL. THERE WAS NOTHING ELSE YOU COULD DO IN THE CIRCUMSTANCES. IN ANY CASE YOU MORE THAN MADE UP FOR IT LATER.

BOB HAD SOMETHING TO TELL THE PAIR HIMSELF. HE HAD TO ADMIT HE'D GOT THE TWO MEN ALL WRONG.

I HAD MY DOUBTS ABOUT YOU, CORPORAL BRADDON AND YET I THOUGHT YOU WERE THE MAN FOR THE JOB, RUSSEL. I THINK THAT THE TWO OF YOU WILL MAKE A PRETTY EFFECTIVE TEAM, THAT'S IF YOU'LL STAY WITH US.

WE'LL STAY, SIR.

AS MIKE AND JOE WALKED AWAY, BOB TURNED TO SEE THAT GEORGE HAD A BROAD GRIN ON HIS FACE. THE CURIOUS LIEUTENANT ASKED WHAT THE CAUSE OF HIS AMUSEMENT WAS.

REMEMBER WHAT I SAID ABOUT WINNING STRIPES, SIR?

IF PROMOTION HAS TO BE EARNED THEN BRADDON'S EARNED HIS A DOZEN TIMES OVER. I REMEMBER, ONLY TOO WELL.

AN EMBARRASSED BOB HAD TO ADMIT THAT GEORGE HAD BEEN RIGHT.

THE COVERS